Becca's Story: Purpose

Finding Herself Series
Book 2

Erica J Whelton

Publisher: Sunseri Design Publishing
ISBN: 978-1-956069-08-2

Printed in the United States of America

This one is dedicated to my children. They helped me through my single mom years and have supported my dream of writing.
Thanks kids!

Table of Contents

People with purpose, goals, and visions have
no time for drama.
They invest their energy in creativity and
focus on living a positive life.
Unknown

Chapter One

"Hi, my name's Becca, and I'm an alcoholic."

I tried not to make eye contact with anyone in the room while remembering to breathe. The folding chair beneath me felt cold and hard, and the fluorescent lights hummed overhead. Everything felt too bright, too exposed.

"It has been two months since my last drink." I paused, swallowing hard. "And I am here doing this for my children. They deserve better."

With tears threatening, I nodded to the room, gave a half smile, then took my seat. Keeping my eyes down, I fidgeted with the hem of my shirt as the next speaker stood.

The meeting went on, and I tried to be engaged, supportive, and get the most I could out of it, but all I could think about was running far away and drowning my feelings in beer or vodka or maybe tequila.

Yes, tequila would be perfect for how I was feeling. A couple of shots and I would forget about my problems, the pain in my hip, and the loneliness I felt daily.

I smiled at the current speaker and tried to focus on what he was saying. He was further along on the journey than me and hadn't fallen quite as far either. It only took his wife threatening to leave him. That was the moment he knew he had to get help.

He'd been coming to these meetings for nearly a year, and it saved his marriage. His words, not mine. His wife smiled up at him from the audience as he spoke, clasping her hands in front of her, mouthing along with him like she'd heard the speech a hundred times and still believed every word.

What did that feel like? Having someone believe in you like that.

On the other hand, it took me being in a life threatening car accident and the worry in my oldest daughter Mandy's eyes to make me realize I'd hit rock bottom. It had only been a few months since, but it had been my wake up call. Unfortunately, I still had a limp to remember it all by.

My ex boyfriend, Butch, had been driving, and we hit a family. It killed all but the youngest member of the family. The youngest boy had survived and was currently living with relatives.

Survivor's guilt would be something I would live with, probably my entire life. Having lost my parents in my early twenties to a car accident, I hated that the boy would grow up without his father, mother, and siblings. I knew that kind of loss. It hollowed you out in ways that never fully healed.

Butch had been in jail since, awaiting trial. No one had been either willing or able to post his bail as it had been set high. I would be testifying against him.

I couldn't wait for that part of my life to be behind me. It had not been a good memory, not just the accident but that whole relationship. What had I been thinking?

My whole life had been a series of bad relationships, but he was the worst. Evil through and through. At this point, I couldn't imagine what I saw in him, but like most of my relationships, he paid my bills, bought me presents, and kept me in alcohol.

I'd never had to work or break into the inheritance my parents had left me. I had most of it left, and if I was careful, I could get by on it for many more years.

After the accident, Mandy sat with me while I was unconscious in the hospital, barely leaving my side. All I had put her through in her life, yet she was still worried and willing to put her life on hold for me. How did I get so lucky? How did she still have it in her to care?

I had gotten pregnant with her when I was only fourteen years old. I had told everyone, including my parents, that I had been raped. That wasn't true. It had almost been, but I knew who the father was. He was the one who rescued me from my would be rapist and was the love of my life. I lost him because I was scared and panicked.

That wasn't an excuse for how I treated my children. I made choices that impacted them all, but Mandy had always gotten the brunt of my wrath. It broke my heart to think of the pain I caused her. Somehow, she turned out to be a sweet, kindhearted person who put others first. No thanks to me.

The meeting started to wrap up, waking me from my reminiscing, so I stood to leave. I folded my chair to put it away, as we were instructed to do at the beginning of the meeting, when I heard someone call my name.

"Becca? So, what did you think of your first meeting?"

My sponsor Rachel was an older lady with a similar backstory as mine. Sadly, she lost custody of her children after an accident in the bathtub that left her son with severe brain damage. She got to see them with supervision a few times a month.

Her son was my Davy's age when the accident occurred, and he was now in his early twenties but had the mental capacity of a toddler. I pictured my Davy like that, and it made me want to work that much harder.

The day before, we'd met so she could share her story and listen to mine. The idea was to have a familiar and friendly face in the group when you arrived. Someone who knew what you'd been through because they'd been through it too.

"Oh, hmm, it was about what I expected. I guess." I fidgeted a little with the chair. I wanted to escape. I wanted a drink. The stronger, the better.

"It's normal to be craving and a little shaky at this point. It will get easier but never fully goes away. At least it never went away for me. I still think about alcohol almost daily." A shadow of sadness seemed to pass over her face but passed quickly, and she was back to supportive sponsor mode. "But eye on the prize. It's worth it. I promise."

"How could you tell? How do you deal with it?"

"You have that look in your eyes, and you're shaking a bit." She gestured towards my hands, so I looked down. I clenched them tight and tried to mentally will them to stop shaking. "Normal for newbies. I just keep thinking of why I wanted to quit. My children. I focus on them. Call me anytime, day or night. I've been there." She squeezed my arm lightly before walking away to speak with someone else.

I finished putting my chair away, smiled at a few members as I walked out, and made my hasty retreat to my car. Once inside, I broke. All the feelings were too much. I had spent most of my life drinking away my feelings, but this new life was about facing them. I didn't know if I was strong enough to face it. Not all at once anyway.

This was going to be tough. Not only this meeting but the whole process of finding myself, recovering from my addiction, and finding purpose in life. I would have to feel it all. The loss of my youth. My parents. Missing out on my children's lives.

Most of the problems were caused by my own choices, but it didn't make it hurt any less. I had especially missed out on Mandy's life. She was grown now. It felt like a blink of an eye, and I had thrown it all away.

That was enough pity party for one night. Nothing I could do about the past. What mattered now was how I handled my future.

The meeting took place roughly fifteen minutes away from Glenn Lake, so I had plenty of time to think and let the tears fall softly into the darkness of the evening.

I wiped a few tears from my face, though it was pointless. For every one I wiped away, two more took its place. Taking a deep breath, I put the car in drive and pointed it towards home, and my brain picked up the memories where I had left off.

Physically my body had nearly healed. The doctors were surprised by my progress. It was just a few months since the accident, and I was almost back to normal. I had the limp, and occasionally I had pain in my hip, but aside from that, I was completely recovered.

The battle now was all mental. I had to work to live without alcohol and learn to be an adult and a mother to my younger two children. Missy would be five soon, and Little Davy was nearly three. They were both growing up so fast.

I had missed out on all the baby stuff. Mandy had handled it while I was too busy drowning my sorrows. She had been an excellent caregiver to them. I don't know how she had it in her, considering I had been the worst example of a mother.

Then, of course, there was Mandy herself. What could I say about Mandy except, how do you live in the shadow of your own child?

She had practically raised herself. She was eighteen going on thirty with a thriving business that employed two employees, three including herself. She raised her siblings, cared for the household, and ensured they had food, clothes, and love. Oh, and ensuring that my messes got cleaned up. That girl was a saint. I didn't deserve her.

I was slightly jealous and yet proud of all she had done with her life and for her siblings. She had everything. Granted, things hadn't always gone her way. But she had worked hard to get where she was, and no thanks to me at all. I was a deadbeat. I admit it. But all I could do was move forward and try to do better.

I tried when she was first born, but I wasn't ready to have a child. Who at fourteen was? Heck, I didn't even know if I ever wanted to have children. I really thought I would become a lawyer like my father. It had always been my dream, and that dream never included kids.

In my world, my dad was all powerful, and people everywhere respected him. He seemed to just have this aura of power about him. He commanded respect from my mother, from me, and from those around him. When he walked into a room, people stopped talking and watched his every move, trying to emulate him.

I guess I thought if I were a lawyer, I would finally have control and power over my life, and maybe he would eventually love me and be proud of me. When I walked into a room, I got hit or yelled at, and that was just by my father.

My mother mostly ignored me. It was like I was a doll she'd gotten bored with. Her philosophy seemed to be that children were almost an accessory of sorts.

"You sit quietly and don't fidget or draw attention to yourself." She'd tell me this every time we'd have company or if we were going out in public. "Don't embarrass me."

She'd dress me in prim and proper outfits. As a young girl, it was dresses with lots of lace and ruffles. Later, clothing that made me look like a miniature businesswoman. Pantsuits with pearls or pleated skirts and pumps. None of my friends dressed this way.

But secretly, I liked it. It made me feel strong. Powerful.

While some little girls pictured themselves getting married, having babies, and houses with white picket fences, I imagined myself single, living in a hip apartment downtown with a closet full of power suits and heels. I would take on the big, high profile cases, and I would win them all. Then, when I stepped into the courtroom, the opposing lawyer would curse and know they had already lost.

Instead, I threw my life away by getting pregnant at fourteen and then spent the next nearly eighteen years of my life drinking until I was stupid and angry. My wardrobe mainly consisted of leggings or jeans with oversized tees or tank tops. I didn't even own a pair of heels. I really didn't need them in my current life of doing nothing.

The only truth to my whole fantasy life was that I was currently single. I was the worst at picking guys. Sober and remembering, I could only shake my head at my poor choices. The abuse I put both myself and Mandy through had me wishing I could erase my past from my mind. Instead, it hit me all at once, blow after blow, as I remembered the losers. Their faces flashed through my mind like a slideshow of mug shots.

"Blah! Stop." I chastised myself. "Think of something else."

The only men in my past that had been worth a thing were the fathers of my children. My face softened as I thought of them both. I hadn't seen Mandy's father in eighteen years, not since I ended things with him. He had always been my savior with his kind heart and generous nature.

I'm sure that's why Mandy had turned out so well. Because of her father's good, kind heart and his strength of spirit.

Sadly, Mandy's father didn't even know about her. If he'd known, he would have done right by her and me. Which is precisely why I had to end it. He would have thrown his dreams away.

Instead, he became the first in his family to go to college. There was no way I was going to be the one standing in his way.

He had saved me from myself time and time again, and for that, I was forever grateful to him. Yet I had avoided him, lied to him, and kept his child away from him. Yes, I had been an awful person. Again, onward and upward was my new motto for how I was going to live.

I pulled into the driveway and could see that, for the most part, the house was dark, except for a low light in the living room. Mandy, no doubt, was working. I don't know how she does it or where she got her work ethic. Not from me, that's for sure. I never held down a job for more than a few weeks at a time.

I couldn't help but smile, thinking of my firstborn and her remarkable work ethic. I reached over and grabbed my purse, then got out of the car to head in. Reaching the door, I took a deep breath, smoothed my hair, and plastered on a smile so she didn't know my true feelings.

As I stepped into the house, I saw my assumption was right. Mandy was working. She was video chatting with her two employees, going through their weekly schedule of clients.

"Hi, Mama. How did it go?" Mandy said, looking up with a smile.

"Hi, it was okay."

"Hi, Ms. Becca." Both Claire and Hayley said in near unison.

"Hey, ladies." I waved to the faces on the screen. "I don't mean to disturb y'all."

"No, you're fine. We are wrapping up."

"I'll go start some tea." I nodded towards the kitchen, leaving the girls to get back to discussing clients and scheduling.

I put water in the teapot and started it to boil. Then I pulled out two mugs, added a teabag and a little bit of sweetener to each.

While I waited on the water to boil, I messaged my best friend, Stephanie.

Still good for lunch tomorrow?

She had recently had a baby, and her social life had become unpredictable. He was the cutest little guy with chubby little cheeks and curly blonde hair. He looked a lot like Doug, her husband, but with Steph's smile.

She replied, and we had a brief exchange.

So far, so good!

Great. See ya at Ron's

Perfect. I am craving one of his club sandwiches

Me too! xoxo

<3

Stephanie is my oldest and dearest friend. She has always supported me. When my parents kicked me out, she talked her parents into taking me in. I didn't stay long with them, though. They treated me so well, but I didn't want to burn a bridge by taking advantage of them. I would stay with them as a last resort when other places fell through and I had no other choices.

Not long after Mandy was born, I moved from Glenn Lake to Houston, where I felt I could blend in better, and nobody knew me. I had better access to government assistance, and with the help of a friend, I got a fake ID. It opened even more doors that helped us survive those early years.

I'd been able to rent us an apartment but in an awful part of town. We were all alone, and my parents had made it clear they would not help me in any way.

If you asked me how I made my way during those early years, I couldn't tell you. I did what it took to survive, just my child and me. It's all a blur, and honestly, I'm not proud of some of the things I had to do and don't want to remember, so I blocked it from my mind both through alcohol and pure willpower.

I only moved back to town after my parents had a car accident that killed my father and left my mother disabled. Becoming my mother's caregiver was a low point in some ways. As she had my entire life, she mostly ignored me. Only acknowledging me out of necessity because of her injuries and failing health.

She didn't even admit that she had a grandchild. She never spoke to or about Mandy. It broke my heart, knowing I had been such a colossal disappointment to my parents and that Mandy lost out on that relationship in the process.

It had been like that my entire life. I don't remember being hugged, kissed, or told I was loved. On a good day, I was completely ignored. I tried not to think about the bad days. They provided clothes, shelter, and food, but it was more for appearances and obligation than a desire to be parents. No wonder I didn't know how to do this mom thing, and I drank like a fish.

Later, after my mom had passed and I was left with the house, Steph and I would party and get drunk together. It felt like freedom and youth. I felt like I was on top of the world. No one to answer to. No rules. Parties would last for days. People were always coming in and out, and it was me and my bestie.

That was until she met Doug a few years ago. She quit drinking. She quit hanging out as much with me. They bought a craftsman a few streets over. It needed a lot of TLC, so they renovated it themselves. They got married and now had little Samuel, who was six months old.

Despite getting her life on track and not continuing the partying lifestyle, she still had my back. If I got in trouble, she was there. If I needed to talk, she was there. She was the only other person who knew the truth about Mandy's father. She nursed my broken heart when I broke things off with him years before. Then when he left town shortly after, I cried for months. She was there holding my hand and encouraging me to move forward.

As much as I owed it to myself and my kids to stay sober, I owed it to her. She deserved to have a friend that gave as much to the friendship as she did.

"So, tell me about the meeting?" Mandy grabbed the mugs of hot tea as she came to sit across from me at the table.

"Oh, there isn't much to tell. Everyone introduced themselves. A few shared their stories of success. And there were cookies." I flashed her a fake smile.

She returned the look, which made us both laugh. This was just something silly we sometimes did, at least since my return home.

"Cookies are good. So, how do you feel about the rest of it?" She sipped her tea.

"I feel okay about it. I can tell this won't be easy, but I really want this. For you kids."

"I want this for you too, Mama." She reached over, squeezing my hand.

"Thanks, baby." I returned the squeeze with a smile.

"Well, I have a busy day tomorrow. Four houses and a new client consultation. Good night." She touched my shoulder as she walked past me. It felt nice.

"Good night, baby. Sleep tight."

After Mandy went to bed, I was alone with my thoughts again. This is what scared me most. Having time to think. My head was a mess of guilt and regret, and sleep never came quickly.

I had so many abusers, and nightmares came every night. I never knew which face would hover above me, fists raised, or which voice would be screaming insults. Haunting. I hated to sleep.

I headed to the living room and grabbed the remote. Maybe there was something to keep my mind just busy enough that I didn't have to think. I settled on the Food Network. You couldn't beat an episode of Chopped to keep your brain at the right level of busyness and relaxed. Halfway through the second episode, I fell asleep.

Chapter Two

Thankfully, I'd had a dreamless, peaceful night. No dream faces screaming at me. No imaginary hands hitting me or forcing me to touch them in places I didn't want to think about. The last thing I remember was waiting to find out who would be chopped in the second round and then next, hearing Missy and Little Davy whispering.

"Don't wake Mama up, Davy."

"I not... I be quiet."

They both jumped when I stirred. Oh, stab me in the heart with guilt. I hated that they were afraid of me. Missy had been so loving and attentive when I first got home. I couldn't think of a time recently when I'd been upset or mad. I'm not sure what changed for them. Maybe memories of their evil mom resurfacing?

"It's okay, babies. I'm awake." I smiled at them.

"Sorry, Mama, we tried to be quiet."

"You didn't wake me up. Come give me hugs."

I reached towards them. They hesitated and looked at each other like they were trying to decide what to do. My heart cracked watching that silent conversation between them. Missy gave in first, but Little Davy held back. I don't blame him. His last real memory of me was when I hit him and screamed in his face. The memory haunts my dreams, waking me up with a start each and every time.

I wish I could take that back. He was just a baby. I didn't want him to be thirty two wondering why his mom never loved him. The reality was, I loved him very much. All of my children. I was just rotten at showing it. As part of this new me, I was learning how to figure out who I was and how to act without alcohol.

Affection was something new to me. My parents rarely showed me any, or each other, for that matter. They were both cold, prudish type people. It is a wonder I was even conceived, but no surprise that I was an only child.

When Mandy was born, I was so in love with her. My baby. She was beautiful, and I couldn't believe I'd created someone so perfect. I hugged and kissed her all the time, telling her I loved her, but once I got so deep into the alcohol, it stopped.

Missy and Davy never had that affection from me. I loved them, but I was so marinated in booze and caught up in my own misery.

Now that my mind was clearing and less focused on drinking, partying, and my own selfish endeavors, I had a lot of work to do. This was all new territory for us, and we were learning. I was going to lead by example and be patient. My therapist had tried to assure me several times that they could bounce back with patience and love. It was just going to take a lot of patience and work on my part.

"Are you ready for school? Did you have breakfast?"

"We just ate. Mandy made us eggs and toast."

"Yummy, yummy." Davy rubbed his stomach.

I smiled at my sweet boy.

"Do y'all want me to take you to school?"

Even though I was home, we kept them both in daycare because they enjoyed it and it helped Davy develop his speech. Missy would be starting kindergarten in the fall, so being in this preschool program was getting her ready. She was extremely smart and already reading, thanks to her big sister.

"Umm, I need to ask Mandy." She looked over her shoulder towards the kitchen.

Another little stab. She needed permission to let me be her mother.

"Ask me what?" Mandy walked in as if on cue.

"If Mama can take us to school."

"Of course she can. Why not?" She smiled at me.

I think she felt the kids' shift too. Old habits. She encouraged them to look at me in the mom role as it should be.

"Okay, we'll go get our shoes. Come on, Little Davy." She said brightly, skipping off with Davy behind her.

"Shoes, shoes, shoes... going to get my shoes." He sang down the hall.

"Thanks. I guess we're all still adjusting," I said.

"Yeah, I thought they were getting it, but it looks like we took some steps back. They'll get there." She hugged me. That was nice and needed. "Well, I'm going to head out. Tell Steph I said hi, and I want to see little Sammy soon."

"I'll tell her. Have a good day. Love you, baby."

"Love you too, Mama." She smiled at me as she grabbed her purse and keys before walking out the front door.

A smile tugged at my lips as I stared at the door, thinking how proud I was of her.

Missy and Davy came back in just after Mandy left. They had their backpacks and shoes on.

"Well, let's hit the road."

Their school was only a few minutes away, but I tried to make the drive fun by pretending the car was a spaceship and we were in space. I asked the kids what they saw.

"Oh, stars... The moon... An astronaut!"

"An elephant!" Davy added.

I don't think Little Davy understood the game. His innocence warmed my heart. Maybe I didn't completely mess him up.

Despite his lack of understanding, the game had been fun, and we were laughing by the time I pulled up at their school. They both seemed more relaxed around me as well. They held my hands as we walked to each class and gave me a hug before I left them.

Those hugs. I held onto them a little longer than necessary, memorizing the feel of their small arms around my neck. These were the moments I had missed. These were the moments I was fighting to keep.

But once I had them each in their respective classrooms, I was alone again, at least until it was time to meet Stephanie. This is where I suffered. I hated being alone. It meant feelings and memories.

To keep busy, I decided to stop in at the store. Maybe I could get some bananas to make banana bread. We needed a few other things anyway, so I could get that all knocked out this morning.

"Hello, Becca. How're you doing today?" You have to love small towns where you walk in the store and are greeted by name and by the owner.

"Good morning, Mr. Donovan. I'm well. How are you?"

"Feeling good. How are the kiddos?"

"Great. I just dropped them at school. I was wondering, do you have some overripe bananas?"

He almost always had some. You just had to ask, and he knew exactly how overripe I needed them to be.

"As a matter of fact, I do. I'll go grab it for you." He headed to the back. While he was gone, I grabbed some grapes, a head of romaine lettuce, broccoli, and a couple of onions.

"Making your famous banana bread?" He said, handing me the bananas.

"Yes, that's the plan," I said cheerfully.

"I would pay for a loaf of that!"

"I'd be happy to drop some off for you later, but I would never charge you."

"All righty-roo. Thanks."

We talked for a minute about his schedule so I knew what time would be good to drop back by.

"Mrs. Donovan is going to be so excited to hear. She loves your banana bread too."

I grinned and got back to my shopping. I needed a few more things for the banana bread plus the few items on our shopping list like a gallon of milk, some eggs, a box of the kids' favorite cereal, and some chicken breasts.

Once home, I unloaded the groceries and checked the clock. Plenty of time for a few batches of banana bread. I mixed the batter for the banana bread and got four pans worth in the oven.

We'd keep one. One for our wonderful neighbor, Ms. Graham. And of course, the one I promised the Donovans. The fourth would go to Jimmy when he dropped the little kids off later.

Despite being the father of my two younger children, he and Mandy were dating now. It sounds complicated, but it actually works. They're perfect together. I think I got in the way of fate years ago, and now it was finally sorting itself out. His kids are her siblings, her mother is his ex. A typical American family with a twist.

While that cooked, I cleaned up my mess in the kitchen, then started some laundry. After that, I wandered around a little bit, picking up this stray item here or there. For the most part, we kept the house clean. Much cleaner than when I was drinking.

It used to look like a 24/7 keg party with empty beer cans, vodka bottles, cigarette butts, discarded pizza boxes, and sometimes other things. I shuddered as I remembered that I would blame Mandy and scream at her to clean up, but it wasn't her mess to clean. Still, she would do it without complaint.

Soon she began doing it before I even got upset or yelled. I would wake up after a night of drinking to find a nearly spotless house. It was another thing on the list of items that made her a saint.

After the chores were done, I checked the loaves. They were perfect. Golden brown and fragrant, filling the kitchen with warmth. I put them on the cooling racks so they could start cooling. I needed them cool enough to wrap up for delivery.

"Ugh, now what do I do?"

Maybe I should think about getting a job or a hobby, or perhaps we needed a dog. No, I don't need to take care of anything else right now. I needed to focus first on my recovery.

I flipped through a few social media sites. Nothing special, but it passed the time. Finally, I checked on the loaves. They were cool enough to wrap, and it was finally time for me to get going anyway.

First, I ran next door to deliver a loaf to Caroline. The little kids called her Grammy since her last name was Graham. She was like a grandmother to all three of them, and she loved them as if they were her own. I had known her my whole life, and she held a special place in my heart. She always had our backs.

"Oh, hello, dear. What brings you by?" Caroline Graham said, answering the door.

Always the picture of posh, she was wearing her silvery white hair in a perfect French twist and wearing a crisp peach blouse and navy slacks, and around her neck, a single strand of pearls.

"I made banana bread. Mr. Donovan wanted some, so I thought I would share the love." I handed her the still warm loaf.

"Well, isn't this a nice surprise? Bless Rich and his sweet tooth. Do you have time for tea?"

"I wish I did. I'm going to deliver this loaf to him at the store and then meet Stephanie and little Sammy for lunch."

"That sounds lovely. Well, you run along. I'll be visiting the Daileys later. Poor Norm has not been doing well again, so I'm going to cheer up Frannie. I can share with her. Thank you so much."

"Give my love to Norm and Frannie." I waved as I walked down the stairs.

I drove into town, stopping first by the grocery to drop off the banana bread for Mr. Donovan. He was thrilled and thanked me, trying again to give me money. I laughed and declined.

After leaving Mr. Donovan, I drove around the square to park near Big Ron's, but of course, there were no spots in front of the diner. I had to go down a block and across the street. There was a big festival in Galveston this weekend, and even though it was more than thirty miles away from us, Glenn Lake always managed some of the overflow tourists.

We were a quaint, small town with funky shops, quirky boutiques, and dusty antique stores that were a draw for tourists. We had incredible restaurants that had become must try places, like Mary's Bakery or Big Ron's Diner.

Then, of course, there was Glenn Lake Park. The lake was the main attraction, and the city kept it nice and stocked with fish. There were nice walking trails around the lake, well maintained playground equipment and splash pads for the kids, and a recently added dog park with sections for different sized dogs and splash pads for the dogs to cool off in.

In recent years, the town had been featured on several travel sites, blogs, and a few magazines as a must visit spot in this region. Plus, the various travel shows or food network type shows came and featured many places around town. It was good for business, but sometimes the charm of Glenn Lake was gone.

Thankfully, it wasn't always overflowing with tourists. It was typically one of those safe Mayberry types of towns where everyone watched out for each other, knew each other, and you could, for the most part, leave your front door unlocked.

I had to dodge a few families as they made their way around our little town. Probably heading to Mary's Bakery for a cookie or Tara's for a scoop of homemade vanilla ice cream with sprinkles.

Maybe the mom would poke around one of the many boutique stores, looking for the perfect one of a kind blouse or artisan jewelry. The dad might be a reader and find something in the used bookstore. After a snack and shopping, they might head to Glenn Lake Park to enjoy the scenery and run off some energy.

As I crossed the street and the front of Big Ron's came into view, so did a familiar face. Not one I had seen in many years. Not since I was fifteen years old when he'd left for college. Ricky Torres.

Oh my, he looked fantastic. Much like his younger self, yet an older and wiser version.

His jet black hair was short. He preferred it short to keep it under control. I actually loved it when he had let it grow out a little, and I could play with his wavy curls. He still looked fit but softer, not as hard muscle, like when he'd played football.

My heart skipped a beat. I was fifteen again. My Ricky. My body tried to pull me forward towards him.

Oh crap. I snapped back to reality. He couldn't see me. I looked around for a place to hide or a way to get past him without him seeing me. I had to get to the restaurant and didn't want to speak to him. But it was too late. Just as that thought crossed my mind, he saw me.

"Becca? Becca Morgan? Oh my gosh, it is you!"

"Ricky? Oh, wow, how are you?" Be calm. Act natural.

"I'm good. I'm good. How are you? You look great." He let his eyes take in my whole five-foot three-inch frame. A chill ran through me.

"Oh, thanks. I'm well. You look great too. Are you visiting?"

"No, I moved back to town. My children and I did." The door of Big Ron's opened, and out walked a girl about eight, followed by a younger girl. When the older of the two looked up at me, my heart stopped.

She looked exactly like Mandy had at that age.

The same dark hair. The same suspicious eyes. The same tilt of her chin. It was like looking at a ghost of my daughter's childhood.

I gasped.

"Are you okay?"

"Yeah, sorry. I thought... Hi." I said that last part to his girls, trying to recover.

"Becca, these are my daughters Amelia and Darla. Girls, this is an old friend of mine, Ms. Becca."

"Hello, Ms. Becca," Amelia said, eyeing me. She was suspicious like Mandy too. Did she sense something? Could she tell just by looking at me that I was connected to her somehow?

"Hiya, Ms. Becca!" Darla grinned up at me. She had a bubbly and bouncy energy about her. She moved just enough that her dress twirled slightly around.

"Nice to meet you both."

"Well, we better get going. I left my son over at the restaurant with my mom, but we need to catch up soon."

"Definitely," I said as he leaned over, giving me a hug.

His arms around me. After all these years. I wanted to melt into him and never let go. Instead, I stood stiff as a board.

Was that my imagination, or did Amelia just give me a dirty look?

"We'll get together soon to catch up. Take care." Then he gathered his girls, and they were gone.

I stood there watching them walk away. Darla turned around, flashing me a bright smile and giving me a little wave. I returned the gesture. Amelia saw her and gave me yet another dirty look.

I had heard his wife had died last year. Cancer. She was, perhaps, in her early thirties when she passed. Too young.

I didn't know he had moved home. That was news. I would have to remember that and really watch where I went. I did not want to run into him again, at least not a surprise run in like this. I was completely caught off guard. Old feelings started to bubble up. Both good and bad. The happiness of being in love. The heartache of ending things. And the loneliness of every day without my soulmate.

I had been so careful over the years not to run into his family. I avoided places I knew they would be, and except for school, I kept Mandy pretty much away too. I know she had gone to school with some cousins, but I couldn't keep her home. I had just hoped nobody would notice, and from what I could tell, they hadn't.

She had gotten invited to a couple of birthday parties over the years. Unfortunately, a few had been from her cousins, and I had to tell her no without explanation. Over time, she stopped getting any invitations at all. She was the girl without friends. The weird girl. At the time, I didn't care about anything but Ricky's family not finding out about her. I wasn't strong enough then to face all the questions.

Was I now?

My cell phone's ringtone startled me awake from my trip down memory lane. It was Steph.

"Hey, girl. Are you here?"

"Yep, I just parked. Can you help me with Sammy?"

"Of course. Where are you?"

I walked back across the street to help Stephanie. She had parked in the opposite direction from me.

"Hi, little Sammy baby." She handed him to me as soon as I walked up, then she grabbed the diaper bag and her purse. "Oh, he has gotten so big! I can't believe how fast they grow. I just saw you last week, wasn't it?"

"Yes, he's growing like a weed. Did I tell you he is crawling?"

"No! Oh Sammy, are you crawling already?" He cooed at me and smiled a big gummy smile.

"So guess who I just bumped into. You'll never guess."

"Ricky Torres?"

"Wait? How did you know?"

"Wild guess, and I was at Abuelita Carmen's last night. He was our waiter."

"What? Why are you just now telling me?"

"I thought you knew. He has been home for a month now. Plus, I'm just now seeing you."

I just stared at her for a second. "You could have messaged me."

I couldn't believe everyone knew but me. Then again, I had avoided the whole Torres family, which included a boycott of the most popular restaurant in Glenn Lake because his family owned it. It was named for his great grandmother, who still worked there. She made all the tortillas for the restaurant. I missed those tortillas. I sometimes had Stephanie buy some and bring them to me.

"You really didn't know?"

"No, I didn't. I just can't believe it. I am shocked."

We walked into Big Ron's and were seated quickly. Our waitress was Nancy. The three of us had gone to school together and had been friends until I got pregnant. She took a different path in life.

"Hey, girls. Hey, little Sammy. Two iced teas?"

"Hi Nancy. Yes, that's what I would like. Becca?" Steph wiped some drool off of Sammy's mouth. I forgot how much babies did that. It was adorable.

"Yes, same. Thanks, Nancy." I smiled up at her. "I think we are both ready to order as well, yes?" I gestured to Stephanie.

"Yes, a club sandwich with fries."

"Same."

"Good choice, ladies. My fave too." She smiled and whirled around to go put in our order.

After she had gone, Steph and I caught up on the past few days of life. I told her about my first AA meeting and how counseling was going.

"Well, it sounds like the meeting went as expected." She said. "Do you feel good about it?"

"I do. I think this is the right step forward. Finally."

"I'm glad. You had us all so scared."

"I know." I hated talking about me. "So, tell me, what's going on with you? What fun project do you have going on?"

Their house was always a work in progress. It looked amazing to me, but Steph was a wannabe house flipper and was using her house as practice until they could buy a house to actually flip.

"Oh, well, Doug just finished some landscaping. He planted a beautiful new oak sapling."

Doug was her husband and, in my opinion, a good sport with all the projects Steph volunteered him for.

When they first moved in, they had renovated it and loved it. But she'd get new ideas and just have to try them out. Take out this wall, put up a wall there, add a window, change the flooring again, and continue the list. You never knew what you would find walking into their house.

Nancy brought our iced teas, chatting briefly with us before leaving to wait on a few other customers. She returned shortly after with our sandwiches. His club sandwiches always hit the spot. Such a simple thing, but something about them was simply perfect and comforting.

We continued chatting about life, laughed a lot, and talked about our kids. Sammy was adorable. He was at a fun age. He liked to play peek a boo and played even when I didn't know we were playing. I had missed this age with my three. I had bits of it with Mandy, but I was so focused on surviving, I didn't enjoy it enough.

Too soon, we had finished our lunch. I helped Stephanie get back to her car. She had to get Sammy home for his nap.

"It was so good to see you again. Next week?"

"Yes, definitely." I gave her a hug and waved as she drove away.

Chapter Three

I stood there looking up one side of the street and down the other. I had a couple of hours before I needed to be home. Jimmy would be picking up the little kids, so I would just need to be home in time to get dinner started. Little Davy would be napping right now, and I know Missy enjoyed reading time, which was always after lunch, so I wouldn't want to disrupt their day anyway. I guess I could go be a Glenn Lake tourist.

I walked up North Main and started poking into some of the little boutique shops. I wasn't looking for anything, just killing time. I knew most of the locals, so I chatted with a few that I bumped into here and there.

I wandered into the used bookstore, thinking maybe I would pick up a new book for myself and perhaps something for the little kids. Mandy had recently gotten a Kindle, so she was reading on that now. I still enjoyed the feel of a book, and you couldn't get that smell from an e-book, though I could see the appeal in having a whole library in your hands. Need a book? A few clicks and it was right there.

Stepping into the bookstore, I was immediately hit with that smell. That wonderful old book smell. A happy warmth spread through me as I headed straight to the mystery books. I loved a good mystery. I scanned the shelves until I found what I was looking for, which turned out to be two books instead of the one I intended to get.

Then I walked over to the children's books. I browsed through the picture books and found a book about a cowboy dog that Davy would love and another about a circus dog. Then I looked through the early chapter books for Missy. Junie B. Jones was her current favorite, so I got her the next two in the series. She would be thrilled.

This was the kind of mom I wanted to be. The kind who noticed what her kids liked and surprised them with little things. The kind who paid attention.

"Hi, Becca."

"Hi, Mrs. Garner. How are you today?"

"I'm good. Thank you, dear." She started to scan the books. "Oh, these are good ones. Nothing like a good mystery."

"I agree."

With the transaction complete, I wished her well and headed back to my car but was stopped by the smell coming from Mary's Bakery. It smelled heavenly. I had banana bread at home and didn't need any more treats. Of course, I could always freeze it.

I looked over my shoulder towards the bakery, knowing I was going to give in and that we'd end up eating the banana bread and whatever baked goods I bought from Mary too.

I turned and made a beeline for the bakery. Pushing through the door, I was met by the smell of fresh coffee and baked goods.

"Hmm... smells good in here, Mary." I eyed the cookies in the case, not even looking up at the baker's sweetly smiling face.

"Thanks, Becca. What can I get for you today?"

I picked out some chocolate chip cookies, two each pink frosted and orange frosted sugar cookies for the little kids. Then a dozen oatmeal raisin for Mandy and me. We were too much alike sometimes. As she rang up the sale, I made small talk with her.

I had always liked Mary. She looked like your typical middle aged mom type. You know, that sweet, quiet type like a modern day Carol Brady. Yet when you talked to her, she was nothing like you would imagine. Mary had a wacky side and told it like it was.

"So, how's your son? Didn't he just get married?"

"Yes, he's doing well. He and his husband are in the process of selling their place. You know he writes that travel blog? Well, he was just offered a year long contract to travel and write about his experiences. I don't understand how all that works or how it makes money, but they are thrilled, so who am I to say anything?"

I didn't want to call her out on my disbelief that she held her tongue. That wasn't Mary's style. However, I am sure they both got an earful of her opinion on the subject.

"That's exciting! I read his blog sometimes. He has a way with words."

"He better. I paid enough for that fancy degree of his. I told him that I wanted to have grandchildren before I died. So, they better get on with figuring out about making money and this adoption process." She gestured wildly as she talked. It was cute.

"Yeah, yeah, get this traveling thing behind them. Fine. But adoptions don't just happen overnight. I told them nobody would take them seriously if they were off gallivanting all over the world. They needed to settle down in one place. Of course, I want them here. Sean grew up here, and I'm here. It only makes sense." She continued with her venting and ranting.

I listened. It sounded like she just wanted to vent and wasn't really looking for a reply, which was good because I didn't know what to say anyway.

I knew Sean. He was a little younger than I was but was a sweet kid. All the girls had a crush on him, but one look and you just knew he was gay. Not sure why some didn't see it. I supposed it was wishful thinking on their part because he was hot for sure, but he was definitely checking out the football guys right along with the girls.

He met Levy in college, but they didn't date until a few years later, having run into each other at an event in New York and never looked back. They had gotten married this past year. I saw pictures on Facebook a mutual friend had shared. It looked like it had been a beautiful reception.

I had met Levy a few times. They were a great match. You couldn't help but smile when you saw them together. One of those couples that you just knew would grow old together.

Gosh, I was jealous. It seemed like everyone was a couple lately. Mandy and Jimmy. Doug and Steph. Sean and Levy. Where was my happily ever after?

Maybe I didn't deserve one. Maybe all those years of bad choices had used up whatever good was meant for me.

A family came into the bakery, no doubt tourists. I waved goodbye to Mary as she started to help the newcomers.

Back on the street, my mind drifted to thoughts of Ricky. Nobody knew how much he meant to me or that he was Mandy's father. I never told anyone except Steph. I can't believe she didn't think to text me immediately when she found out he was in town.

I thought back to when I first met him. It was just a few weeks before I would turn fourteen. The memory came rushing back, as vivid as if it had happened yesterday.

I had finally gotten asked out by Russell Schultz. He was the cutest, most popular boy in our school. He was a few years older, which was fine with me because boys my age were dull.

I had to sneak to see him, telling my parents I would be with Stephanie, which wasn't a complete lie. She was there too.

Russ was throwing a party at his uncle's farm and invited Steph and me. His uncle was not home at the time. He lived in Houston and only came to Glenn Lake on weekends. This was summer and a weekday, so it was the perfect place for kids to drink, smoke, and have sex.

I had too much to drink, and Russell took advantage of that fact. He got me alone and tried to pressure me into sex. I refused, but he wasn't taking no for an answer. He ripped my shirt, broke the zipper on my jeans, and then climbed on top of me. I was crying, hitting, and fighting against him.

He was so much bigger than me. I was barely five feet tall and all of ninety pounds if that. He was twice my size and was on the football team. It might have only been the freshman team, but he was built and worked out daily, so he was strong. I was never going to be able to fight my way free, but I wasn't going to quit fighting as long as I could.

I just kept hoping someone from the party would hear me and come save me. Stephanie had to know I was missing and come looking for me. The music was loud, though, so my screams were going unanswered.

He shook me. "Shut up, just shut up, Becca. I know you aren't a virgin, so just drop the act."

"No, no, please, Russ. I don't want to do this. Please, you're hurting me."

He laughed in my face. "If you don't stop wiggling around and just give up already, I will definitely hurt you."

I kept fighting, so he hit me on the side of my head a few times and slammed my head down on the ground a couple of times. I saw stars and heard a buzz in my ears. It took a lot of the fight out of me. I was starting to realize this was going to happen, and I wasn't going to be able to fight him much longer.

Suddenly there was a noise behind us, and he was pulled off of me. I couldn't see very well, but fists on flesh. That sound was unmistakable. I also heard a male voice I didn't recognize telling Russell that isn't how you treat girls or something like that. Things were fuzzy.

I think I might have lost consciousness for a moment because I don't remember how the fight ended or what happened to Russell.

Just that suddenly there was a blanket, a gentle hand, and a soothing voice. I wrapped the blanket around myself to hide my torn clothing. I tried to smile at the stranger. I couldn't see him well enough yet to recognize him. It was dark, and my head was still spinning.

"It is okay now. I ran him off." His face came a little more into focus, and I could see him. It was Ricky Torres. He was a few years older than me, though I didn't know him well.

"Thank you for helping me." I sniffed and tried to stifle my tears.

"Can I help you get home or back to a friend?"

"I... I don't know. I don't know what to do. My parents will kill me if I come home like this, and I don't want anyone at the party to see me like this either."

"Who did you come with? Was it that guy?"

"Yes, but also Stephanie Wilson. Do you know her?"

"I know her brother. I can find her. Let me get you into my car so you are safe. Then I will get Stephanie for you."

He helped me to his car. "I'll be right back. Keep the doors locked until I get back." He returned after a few minutes with a distraught Stephanie. She climbed in the front seat with me. She held me all the way back to her house. We cried the whole way.

I thanked Ricky, and then Steph and I snuck into her house. We threw out my torn up clothes. I showered, got changed into some pajamas, and climbed into her extra bed. After Steph had gone to sleep, I just kept thinking of my knight in shining armor. He was truly my hero.

The memory faded, and I was back on the sidewalk in Glenn Lake, eighteen years later. I had loved Ricky from that moment on. He didn't know it then, but he had saved more than just my body that night. He had saved whatever was left of my hope that good people existed.

And then I had pushed him away. Lied to him. Kept his daughter from him for eighteen years.

Maybe that's why I didn't get a happily ever after. Maybe I had already been given one, and I threw it away.

Chapter Four

It had been a week since I saw Ricky, and I'd been avoiding going back into town since.

The only time I left the house was to take the kids to daycare and then to my counseling sessions and Alcoholics Anonymous meeting, which both took place in other cities.

However, I couldn't put it off any longer and had a few errands to run, including Donovan's grocery store, the bank, and I wanted to stop by Mary's Bakery. Those oatmeal raisin cookies were incredible, and no, they weren't must haves. It was more like I needed more of those cookies.

Why had I never had them before? She added just enough cinnamon that made them warm and comforting to the soul. Maybe they would replace alcohol as my new vice. Okay, perhaps not, but only for today.

I started at the bank. I was nearly done paying off my hospital expenses, but each time I had thought I had paid it all off, another bill from another specialist or department would come in. It was like a never ending cycle. It had been expensive, but thankfully I had money from my parents. I'd just need to move it around between my accounts. It was a small town bank, so it hadn't gotten into many of the online features that larger banks have available.

Honestly, it was amazing that I hadn't drunk it all away, though it was one of my regrets. What it meant was I hooked up with a lot of men. Men that paid for a lot of stuff, mostly the booze. I rarely had to buy my own as there was always a man willing to buy me dinner and a six pack. On occasion, they also would pay some bills for me or buy me some clothes.

My face warmed at the thought. I had traded pieces of myself to survive. Pieces I could never get back. But that was the past. This was a new Becca, so I held my head a little higher as I walked into Glenn Lake Bank.

"Hey, Becca. Good morning." Mr. Mulroney was pouring himself some coffee at the coffee area near the front door.

"Good morning, Mr. Mulroney."

"What can I do for you today?"

"I need to transfer money from my savings to my checking."

"Okay, step over to my office, and I can get that taken care of for you."

I sat in his visitor chair while he typed on his computer. He made some small talk asking about the kids, telling me about his.

"How is Valerie doing?" I asked.

"She's fine. You probably heard she's pregnant."

"I did."

"Baby is due in August." His voice caught in his throat. "She'll finish out this semester and then move back here."

"I'm sure it will be nice to have her close by."

"Yeah, and a grandbaby to spoil." He looked over at a family picture. "We're looking into some online college options so she can finish her degree."

Having been a teen mom myself, I felt for Valerie, but I also knew he'd wanted her to take over the bank from him in the future. Going to college had been part of that plan, and she'd need to be able to support herself and the baby. I hoped she had more support than I did. I hoped her parents didn't make her feel like a burden the way mine had.

"All right. Done. Is there anything else I can do?"

"Nope, I'm all set. Thank you so much for your help."

"You're welcome. Have a good day."

From there, I headed to the pharmacy and then over to Mary's Bakery. She had a few customers in the shop, so I browsed, eyeing the display counter's different sweets. Mary had a plate with sample cookies on it cut into quarters. I grabbed a piece of an oatmeal raisin. Yum.

"Hiya, Becca. Back again?"

"Hey, Mary. Yes, yes... I'm back. Say, do you put cinnamon in these?" I grabbed another oatmeal raisin from her sample plate.

"I do. Good guess. Nobody ever gets that."

"I love baking."

"So, I've heard awesome things about your banana bread. Legendary."

"I wouldn't go that far."

"No, really. In fact, Rich Donovan was here this morning bragging about your banana bread. Said if you ever decided to go into business for yourself, I would have some competition."

"Really?" Interesting.

"Yes, and he asked if I ever considered hiring you and specifically so you can make that banana bread. And, truth be told, I have thought about it but never had a chance to ask you... So whatcha think?"

"What do I think about making banana bread for you? I'd never thought about it before." It was true. Other than being a lawyer, I'd never had any other career aspirations. When the pregnancy test showed positive, plus the two more after that, all hopes of doing anything flew out the window. "You just want me to make banana bread?"

"Well, so what I'm offering is for you to work here with me. You can help me with everything, and you can make your banana bread plus anything else you'd like to introduce."

It sounded amazing. I knew she had two other employees, but they didn't contribute like this as far as I knew. How could I possibly say no?

"Oh, wow, Mary. Yes, I would love to."

Since there weren't any customers in the store, we discussed the hours and days I could work. Then she offered me a reasonable wage. This was amazing.

My counselor had suggested I find a purpose to my days besides going to various meetings and counseling. Mostly I just sat around waiting. Alone and waiting. The empty hours were dangerous for someone like me. Too much time to think. Too much time to crave.

But this? This was something real. Something that was mine. For the first time in my adult life, someone wanted me for a skill I had. Not for my body. Not for what I could give them in a dark room. For something I had created with my own two hands.

I bought a bunch of various treats for the kids before saying goodbye to Mary. I then headed over to Donovan Grocery. I told Rich the good news and thanked him for his part. All he wanted to know was when my banana bread would be available at Mary's.

"I start on Thursday."

"Well, I'll be there bright and early for that delicious banana bread."

"You are good for the ego! Thank you again."

I took my groceries and headed out, waving as I left the store. I wanted to skip back to my car, maybe shout out loud. This was incredible! I couldn't wait to tell Mandy and Steph. They would both be excited for me.

Mandy was home when I got there. It was lunch for her.

"Hey, Mama. Want a sandwich?"

"Sure. Thanks." I smiled. "So, guess what?"

"What?"

"I got a job!"

"Really? I didn't even know you were looking. Where?"

"Mary's Bakery. Can you believe it? I went for cookies and got a job too."

"That's awesome, Mama. Wow! When do you start?"

"Thursday. I have a few appointments on other days, so that was the best day for both of us. She wants me to make banana bread and whatever else I want that she doesn't already have in the store."

Mandy handed me a ham and cheese sandwich with sliced apples. We chatted while we ate. She was excited for me. Of course, she was. I told her I would handle clean up so she could get back to work. It was only fair since she made the sandwiches. Plus, she still had several hours of cleaning to do while I had a whole afternoon of nothing planned.

Once she left, I messaged Steph to let her know. She was thrilled for me as well. Her excitement for me made me proud of myself. It was an unfamiliar feeling.

For so long, my texts to her were cries for help, and only since the accident had they changed to more friendship ones. I'd realized that I had been a horrible friend to her, only taking and not giving. It was part of my recovery to fix all my relationships.

I sat back and smiled. I didn't know if I could contain my excitement, and I was fighting the urge to run through the streets yelling. I found a purpose.

Instead of an embarrassing display, I decided to research new recipes. Several I had always wanted to try, like zucchini bread, pumpkin bread, or perhaps a lemon cake. The possibilities were endless. I found several and saved them to the computer. I printed a few that I wanted to make right away, but it would mean a trip back to the store. So it would have to wait until closer to Thursday.

A few hours later, Jimmy brought the kids home from daycare. I couldn't wait to tell the little kids. They would love me working at Mary's. They had loved the cookies the other day, and I am sure they would have dreams of mom bringing home all kinds of sweet treats. Something they had never had much of growing up.

"Hey, Becca. I heard about the job. That's awesome. I know where I will be buying my banana bread." Jimmy said.

"Thanks. I am excited."

"Mama, guess what?" Missy bounced with excitement. "There was a new girl at school today."

"Oh yeah?"

"Yeah, she just moved here, but her daddy is from Glenn Lake."

Oh, no. No, no, no. It can't be. Please don't let her say what I think she's going to say.

"Her name is Darla. She has a big sister and a little brother, just like me. Except her sister is eight years old. Her name is Amelia, and her brother is Tomas. I'm going to invite her to my birthday party. She and Olive are my best friends."

"Oh, wow, that's nice." My insides were twisting, and the room started to spin. Of all the kids in that daycare, my daughter had to become best friends with his daughter.

"Mama, are you okay?" Mandy was eyeing me. She knew something was wrong.

"Oh, yes, I'm fine. I just must be tired from all the excitement of the day."

"Well, why don't we go out to dinner tonight?"

"Please, Mama, please?" The little kids begged.

"Where do you want to go?"

"Abuelita Carmen's, maybe? We never go there, and everyone says it is good."

My stomach dropped. His family's restaurant. Of course.

"No, why don't we go over to the Cactus? Y'all love the tacos there."

They all agreed. I dodged a bullet, but how long could I put this off? Soon, I'd have to tell my biggest secret to the two people who could be most hurt by it.

But for tonight, I'd go and enjoy a nice dinner with my family and try not to think about Ricky.

Try being the key word.

Chapter Five

Two more days until my first day at Mary's, and I couldn't sleep. I lay in bed staring at the ceiling, my mind racing through everything that could go wrong. What if I burned the bread? What if nobody bought it? What if Mary realized she'd made a mistake hiring me?

I reached for my phone on the nightstand. It was almost eleven, but Rachel had said to call anytime. I hesitated, my thumb hovering over her number. She probably had her own life, her own problems. She didn't need me bothering her.

But that was the old Becca talking. The one who never asked for help until it was too late. The one who drowned her fears in vodka instead of facing them.

I pressed call.

She answered on the third ring. "Becca? Everything okay?"

"Yeah, I'm sorry to call so late. I just... I couldn't sleep."

"That's what I'm here for. Talk to me. What's going on?"

I told her about the job at Mary's, how excited I was but also terrified. How I hadn't worked a real job in years. How I was scared I would mess it up like I messed up everything else.

"Becca, listen to me." Her voice was calm and steady. "Fear is normal. It means you care about something. The old you didn't care about anything except where the next drink was coming from. This fear? It's healthy."

"It doesn't feel healthy. It feels like I'm going to throw up."

She laughed softly. "That's the butterflies. They'll settle once you get started. Just focus on one thing at a time. Make the bread. Serve the customers. Smile. You can do those things, right?"

"Yeah. Yeah, I can do those things."

"And if you feel overwhelmed, what do you do?"

"Call you."

"That's right. I'll have my phone on me all day. You're not alone in this, Becca."

I felt tears prick my eyes. "Thank you, Rachel. I don't know what I'd do without you."

"You'd figure it out. But you don't have to. That's the whole point."

We talked for a few more minutes about my upcoming AA meeting and how the kids were adjusting. By the time I hung up, I felt calmer. By the time I hung up, the knot in my chest had loosened. Not completely at peace, but calmer. Enough to close my eyes and actually drift off.

The next morning, I woke up early to start preparing. I needed to pick up a few last minute supplies from Donovan's before I could start baking. The list was short: more vanilla extract, another bag of walnuts, and some parchment paper.

I dropped the kids at daycare, giving them each an extra-long hug. Missy looked at me funny.

"Mama, why are you squeezing so hard?"

"Because I love you, that's why."

"I love you too, but I can't breathe."

I laughed and let her go. "Have a good day, baby. I'll see you this afternoon."

Donovan's was quiet when I walked in. Just a few early morning customers grabbing coffee and newspapers. Mr. Donovan waved from behind the counter.

"Big day tomorrow, right? You ready?"

"As ready as I'll ever be. Just need a few more things."

"Well, you know where everything is. Holler if you need help."

I grabbed a basket and headed down the baking aisle. I was comparing vanilla extracts when I heard a familiar voice behind me.

"Becca?"

I turned around. Ricky was standing there with a gallon of milk in one hand and a box of cereal in the other. He looked just as surprised to see me as I was to see him.

"Ricky. Hi." My cheeks warmed.

"Hey. Shopping for the big day? I heard you're starting at Mary's tomorrow."

"Word travels fast in this town."

"Always has." He smiled, and it was the same smile I remembered from when we were kids. The one that made his eyes crinkle at the corners. "I'm really happy for you, Becca. That's exciting."

"Thanks. I'm nervous, honestly."

"You'll do great. I remember you used to bake for me back in the day. Those chocolate chip cookies?" He closed his eyes like he was savoring the memory. "Man, those were good."

I laughed. "You remember those? I burned half of them."

"Yeah, but the ones that weren't burned were amazing."

"You're being generous."

"I'm being honest." He shifted the milk to his other hand. "Hey, do you have time for a coffee? There's that little spot across the street. The kids are with my mom, and I don't have to be anywhere for a bit."

I should have said no. I had baking to do, supplies to buy, a million things on my to do list. But standing there looking at him, I couldn't bring myself to turn him down.

"Sure. Yeah, I'd like that."

We paid for our things and walked across the street to the coffee shop. It was a newer place that had opened since I'd been keeping my head down, avoiding the world. We ordered at the counter and found a small table by the window.

"So," he said, wrapping his hands around his mug, "it's been a long time."

"Eighteen years."

"Eighteen years." He shook his head. "Where did it go?"

"I don't know. I wasted most of mine." I looked down at my coffee. "I'm not proud of how I spent those years, Ricky."

"Hey." He waited until I looked up at him. "We've all got things we're not proud of. What matters is what you do now."

"That's what my therapist says."

"Smart therapist."

We sat in comfortable silence for a moment. It was strange how natural it felt to be sitting across from him again. Like no time had passed at all, and also like a lifetime had passed.

"Do you remember that night at the lake?" he asked. "After the homecoming game?"

I couldn't help but grin as the memory played through my mind. "When you tried to impress me by skipping rocks and fell in?"

"I didn't fall in. I... lost my balance."

"You fell in. You were soaking wet."

"And you gave me your jacket."

"It was freezing that night. I couldn't let you catch pneumonia."

"I still have that jacket, you know."

I stared at him. "You do not."

"I do. It's in a box somewhere. Couldn't bring myself to throw it away."

Something fluttered in my chest. After all these years, he had kept my jacket. It shouldn't have meant so much, but it did.

"I thought about you," I said quietly. "Over the years. I wondered how you were doing, if you were happy."

"I thought about you too." His voice was soft. "More than I probably should have, considering I was married."

"Ricky..."

"I loved Sonya. I really did. She was a good woman and a wonderful mother. But there was always a part of me that wondered what happened to you. Why you ended things the way you did."

I looked away, out the window at the people walking by. If only he knew. If only I could tell him right now, in this quiet coffee shop, before everything got complicated.

But I couldn't. Not yet. Not like this.

"I was young and stupid," I said. It wasn't a lie, just not the whole truth.

"We were both young." He reached across the table and touched my hand. Just briefly, just a moment. "I'm glad you're doing better, Becca. I really am."

"Thank you." My voice came out thick. I cleared my throat. "So, tell me about your kids. Amelia seems... intense."

He laughed, and the heaviness lifted. "That's one word for it. She's protective. She was really close to her mom, and losing her has been hard. She's not great with new people right now."

"That's understandable."

"Darla's the opposite. She's never met a stranger. And Tomas is just along for the ride. He's eighteen months and thinks everything is hilarious."

"Missy and Darla have become quite the pair at daycare."

"So I've heard. Darla talks about Missy constantly. And Olive. The three musketeers, apparently."

"That's what we call them too."

We talked for another hour. He told me about his years in Austin, teaching high school math, meeting Sonya, building a life. He mentioned he'd be starting at Glenn Lake High in the fall, coming full circle back to where he grew up. He told me about her diagnosis, her fight, her death. I told him about my parents, coming back to Glenn Lake, the drinking, the accident. I didn't tell him everything. Not yet. But I told him enough.

When we finally stood to leave, I felt lighter than I had in years.

"Hey," he said as we walked outside, "I'm going to stop by Mary's tomorrow. Show some support. If that's okay."

"I'd like that."

"Maybe bring the kids. Let them see the famous banana bread everyone's talking about."

I laughed. "It's not famous yet."

"Give it time." He looked at me for a long moment. "It's really good to see you, Becca."

"It's good to see you too, Ricky."

We stood there on the sidewalk, neither of us quite ready to walk away. Finally, he nodded and headed toward his car. I watched him go, my heart doing things I hadn't felt it do in a very long time.

I had to tell him. About Mandy. About everything. I couldn't keep this secret any longer, not now that we were reconnecting, not now that he was looking at me like that.

But first, I had to get through tomorrow. First, I had to make it through my first day.

Then I would tell him. I would find the right moment, the right words, and I would tell him the truth.

I just hoped he would still look at me the same way after I did.

Chapter Six

Leading up to my first day of work, I tried out several recipes with mixed results. The kids liked most of them, and I think they could be perfect for the shop with some practice and tweaks to the recipes. I wanted to make a good impression and not give Mary reason to be sorry she hired me. Fingers crossed.

On Wednesday, the day before my first day, I had a counseling session. I was excited to tell my therapist, Lisa, about my new job and that I had found a purpose as she had suggested. I felt like a little kid looking for approval from a parent, and in a way, it was like that.

I sat impatiently in the waiting room, flipping through a magazine but not really reading it. The article I was staring at was about maximizing your small space. Probably helpful information, but I wasn't absorbing any of it with my own distracted thoughts.

Instead of looking at the magazine, I looked at the cheery waiting area. She had a private practice, and it was small. The waiting room only had six chairs and two side tables. The chairs were standard waiting room chairs with a deep purple and black fabric on them. The generic abstract prints on the walls were in most doctor's offices, and the must have fake plant sat in the corner.

There was no receptionist. When you enter, you call an extension on the phone that then plays an automatic message with instructions to wait for her.

When the appointment was over, another door led out to the hallway and bypassed this room. It kept things private.

I set the magazine down and began pacing as I got impatient for my appointment. Then, finally, she came to call me back.

As we settled into her office, each taking our respective seats, she picked up her notepad and pen.

"So, Becca, how was your week since your last appointment?"

"Well, two things. One, I got a job." I paused.

"Oh, that's good news. What kind of job? Tell me about it."

I told her how I had made some banana bread for a few neighbors and friends and how my reputation had made it to the bakery owner.

"That's why she offered me the position."

Lisa made a few notes as I talked, asking questions as needed and then making a few more notes.

"Wow, that's great. I'm glad you have. When do you start?"

"Tomorrow. After I leave here, I plan to go home and make a few dozen loaves of banana bread and a few other flavors. I have everything ready and waiting. I am so excited."

"I'm happy for you. That is what we have talked about with finding purpose in your days. So, what was the other thing?"

"I ran into Mandy's father. He has moved back to town."

"How do you feel about that? Does he know about Mandy yet?"

"I feel... confused. Hopeful. Terrified." I shifted in my seat. "We've actually talked a couple of times now. We ran into each other at the grocery store yesterday and ended up getting coffee. It was... nice. Really nice. Like no time had passed at all."

"That sounds significant. Does he know about Mandy yet?"

"No. Neither he nor Mandy knows. He said he's going to stop by the bakery tomorrow to support me on my first day. He's bringing his kids." I felt my stomach clench. "I keep telling myself I'll find the right moment to tell him, but every time we're together, I just... I can't make the words come out."

"Do you have a plan to tell them?"

"No, not yet. I know I should. I need to. But it's complicated now. We're reconnecting, and it feels good, and I'm scared that once I tell him the truth, he'll hate me. That I'll lose him all over again."

"That fear is understandable, but secrets have a way of coming out on their own terms. It's usually better to control the narrative yourself." She made a note. "What about the other things we discussed? The little kids slipping back into old roles?"

"It's still happening. Me as a stranger and Mandy as the mom. But we're working on it."

"Well, as we've discussed, you need to be consistent and steady. They'll get used to you."

"I know. It's just hard to watch. I was awful to them for their entire lives." I grabbed a tissue so I had something to fidget with.

"What does Mandy think? Is she aware of the digression?"

"Yes, we've talked about it, and she helps to remind them that I'm the mother. They trust her and listen to her."

"That's good. Having her on your side will get them adjusted quicker."

As we wrapped up the session, she gave me homework. I had to tell Mandy and Ricky the truth before my first day at Mary's. She was firm about it. No more waiting for the perfect moment.

"The perfect moment doesn't exist," she said. "You create it by being brave enough to speak."

I promised to work on it, but I was scared.

Scared didn't even begin to cover it. How do you tell your daughter that the father she'd wondered about her whole life was right here in Glenn Lake? How do you tell a man that he has an eighteen year old daughter you kept from him? There were no right words for that. No way to make it okay.

And he was coming to the bakery tomorrow. With his kids. To support me.

I scheduled my next appointment and then drove home to bake lots and lots of banana bread and other flavors of quick bread.

I had plenty of time on the drive, so I thought about how I would tell both Mandy and Ricky about each other. Lisa was right. I needed to do it before tomorrow. I could call Ricky tonight after dinner. I could sit Mandy down and explain everything. I could do this.

But every time I rehearsed the words in my head, they sounded wrong. Hollow. Inadequate.

I had spent her whole life hiding the truth, hiding her, and now I had to come clean. Was I strong enough to face it? It didn't matter. I knew I had to, and I had promised Lisa. Unlike old me, new me planned to keep promises.

By the time I got home, I had convinced myself I would call Ricky after the kids went to bed. I would tell him everything, and then tomorrow, I would tell Mandy. I had a plan.

But then I started baking, and the hours slipped away. I worked all day and part of the evening, getting all my quick breads ready. I had several dozen, mostly banana bread. They were wrapped and waiting for the people of Glenn Lake to try them.

I told myself I would call him once I finished. Then I told myself it was too late to call. Then I told myself I would tell him in person, that it would be better that way. Then I told myself a hundred other lies to avoid doing the thing I knew I needed to do.

With all the anticipation and excitement, I had trouble sleeping but somehow managed a few solid hours. It would be enough to get me through the day.

Tomorrow. I would tell him tomorrow. Before he came to the bakery. I would find a way.

I dressed in my new light blue polo and khakis that I bought per Mary's instructions to wear a polo and khaki slacks. Next, I put my hair in a high ponytail, laced up my most comfortable tennis shoes, and smiled at my reflection.

"This is going to be fun!" I said to myself.

On the way to drop the kids off at daycare, they made up a song about my new job. Mostly Missy. Davy just copied what she said.

"Mama's a baker. Baking all the day. Bake, bake, bake."

They both sang it to me all the way there.

When we arrived, they clapped and cheered.

"Well, that was a wonderful song, babies. Thank you." I then walked them to their respective rooms, kissed their heads, and wished them a good day.

The love from the kids plus the excitement about the job had me almost skipping back to the car, and I giggled as I drove over to the shop, arriving as Mary was flipping the sign over. She waved as she saw me walking up.

"Good morning, Becca. Are you ready for this?"

"Good morning, Mary." I greeted as I stepped into the shop. "Yes, I think I am. I come bearing cake. I have several aluminum pans full of sweet, yummy quick bread. Mostly it is banana, but I have a half dozen each of zucchini and pumpkin loaves too. I have more out in the car."

"Oh, these are perfect. I have already cleared a space for them. Just place them here for now." She gestured to a side table near the counter. "Do you need help with the ones in the car?"

"No, thanks. I can get them." I ran back to my car, coming back with another load of pans.

We got them all sliced and placed them in the display case. I pulled out my phone and took a couple of pictures. My work being sold in a shop. I couldn't believe it. I posted to Facebook, Twitter, Instagram, and Snapchat so everyone knew. Finally, I was ready for my first day.

I heard the front door chime, and in came Caroline Graham.

"Good morning, Becca. Mary."

"Good morning, Caroline," I said.

"Oh, good morning, Caroline. How are you this fine day?" Mary said.

"I can't complain. Can't complain at all."

"So, what can we get for you?" Mary put on her salesperson persona.

"I heard that Becca would be selling her banana bread, and I had to run down for a slice plus a cup of coffee."

"You heard correctly. Becca, could you get that for her? If you want to have a seat, Caroline, we'll bring it over to you in a moment."

Warmth spread through me as I picked out a nice looking slice, poured her some coffee, and put both on a tray with some creamer. She had sat near the front window, so I carried the tray over.

"Thank you, dear. This looks amazing."

No sooner did we have her set than in came Mr. Dixon with Mr. Donovan, followed closely by Stephanie with little Sammy in his stroller. Then, a few minutes later, in came the Daileys.

Mr. Dailey was looking better than the last time I saw him. I had heard the treatments were going well. His cancer was in remission for the first time, but he still had good days and bad. Between the chemo and cancer, it had taken its toll on his body, but it hadn't taken his sense of humor.

"Hey, Norm. Hey, Frannie. What can we get you this morning?" Mary greeted.

"We're here for Becca's world famous banana bread, of course." Norm's deep voice filled the shop.

"And coffee, please?" Frannie added.

"Coming right up." Mary nodded to me as I started dishing it up.

They took a seat with Caroline to wait.

Within the hour, nearly everyone I knew in Glenn Lake had come into the shop. Seeing the crowds, tourists also joined, asking what all the buzz was about.

All my quick bread and about half of Mary's cookies and various pastries were gone as it neared lunchtime. She still had plenty of baked goods to sell, but the mob had put a nice dent in things this morning.

"Well, well, my new employee, you just made me a week's worth of profit in one morning. But now we need more to get through the afternoon. I have all the supplies for you, so get your little rear in the back and make Ms. Mary some more of those money cakes."

I couldn't help but laugh. This was the best day.

Over the next few hours, I was pulling more loaves out of the ovens, and as fast as we put it out, it would sell out. Mary had to call Donovan's and place another order for supplies. In the late afternoon, Mandy came in with the kids and Jimmy. They were followed by Kate and Olive.

"Hi, Mama! We came to see you." Missy ran to me.

"Hi, y'all. Thank you for coming to see me."

"We wanna get some cookies and nanana bread." Little Davy grinned and started eyeing the cookies.

He really didn't care about the banana bread. He only had eyes for the cookies.

As they were making their choices, the door chimed, and in came Ricky with his children.

My heart stopped. He had said he would come. He had promised to bring the kids. And I still hadn't told him. I had meant to call him last night, to find a way to tell him before this moment, but I had been so busy baking and then so exhausted and then so scared. And now here he was, walking through the door with a smile on his face, and Mandy was standing right there, and everything was about to fall apart.

My eyes darted around to the various people this would impact. Mandy. Ricky. The little kids, both his and mine. This encounter would not end well.

"Darla!" Missy and Olive ran to her, both hugging her.

"Girls, girls, please, I just saw you at school. Don't mob me. Gosh." She acted like a celebrity being swarmed by fans, but then they all started giggling and hugging.

"Ricky... Hi..." I forced a smile, my voice barely a whisper.

"Hey, Becca. Told you we'd come by." He grinned at me, and my heart shattered knowing what was about to happen. "The kids wanted to see the famous banana bread and..." That's when he saw

Mandy. He looked at her and then at Amelia and then at me. "Becca?" He knew.

The color drained from his face. He was connecting the dots in real time. Mandy's dark hair. Her eyes. The way she tilted her chin. The same features he saw in Amelia every single day.

"Ricky... Ricky, I can explain."

"Daddy?" Amelia grabbed his hand. "Daddy, what's wrong?"

"It's nothing, Mel. I just..." He looked at me again and then to her with a fake smile. "Why don't you go pick out what you might like? And something for Tomas and Darla?"

He put Tomas down, and Amelia took his hand, walking him over to the case to look at the cookies, but she kept looking back at Ricky.

Mandy was watching Amelia with wide eyes, not moving or making a sound since they walked in. She was stark white and staring at her half sister. Oh God, I was not getting out of explaining this. I think Jimmy knew too because he tried to distract Mandy.

Ricky came closer to me and quietly asked, "Is she? Is she mine?"

"Yes, but I can explain. I was scared... And young. I'm sorry."

Sorry. As if that word could cover eighteen years. As if it could undo all the birthdays he missed, the first steps, the first words, the graduations. Sorry was nothing. And he was right. We had sat there yesterday, sharing memories and laughing, and I had every opportunity to tell him. I had chosen not to. This was my fault.

He looked at Mandy, and for the first time, she looked at him. I could see the tears in her eyes. She knew. Oh God, she knew. She ran from the store. Jimmy looked at me, and if looks could kill, well, I would be dead. He headed out of the store after her. He would have some words for me later, I am sure of it, and I definitely deserved to hear them.

Thankfully, the little kids didn't notice, and Amelia seemed to finally be distracted by the cookies, cupcakes, and Tomas. I looked over at Mary and Kate. Both were in shock but tried to just keep the little kids engaged in the treats. Mary picked out their goodies, and Kate got them all seated on the far side of the shop.

"I'm so sorry, Ricky. I really didn't mean to hurt you. I didn't think..."

"Darn right, you didn't think. How could you not tell me I had a child?" He tried to keep his voice low, but the anger and hurt were clear in his tone. He looked over at his young children and then back to me. "When did you know? Before I left?"

"Yes." I bowed my head, not wanting to meet his eyes.

"Wow, just wow. To think I loved you, but you were so selfish as to keep her from me." His voice cracked. "We sat there yesterday, Becca. We talked for an hour. You had every chance to tell me, and you just... you let me walk in here blind."

"Ricky..."

"Daddy? Daddy, what's going on?"

"Nothing, Amelia. Go back and sit down, please. Stay with your brother and sister."

"What did you do to my daddy? I know this is your fault!" And just like Mandy, she ran from the store.

"Oh great. Can you keep an eye on Darla and Tomas?"

"Of course."

He ran after Amelia. I didn't know how to explain this to the little kids. Thankfully, they didn't ask many questions but just kept eating their treats, and the three besties chatted away about this or that drama from preschool. Clearly, pre-K was the happening place to be and was full of enough drama to keep TMZ busy.

Kate and I stood there with them awkwardly, smiling and making small talk. Mary went back to helping customers that came in, occasionally giving me sympathetic smiles.

Finally, Mandy and Jimmy returned, followed a minute later by Amelia and Ricky. He smiled weakly at Mandy, who returned the gesture. Then he gathered his kids to leave, but not before giving me one final look. It was definitely a look of pain, hurt, and anger.

Jimmy gathered up Missy and Little Davy. Kate said her goodbyes, giving Mandy an extra long hug. Then I was standing there with just Mandy.

"I can explain... I was young. I was stupid. I was..." I let out a heavy sigh.

"So, he is?" She choked a little as if she couldn't get the whole question out.

"Yes."

"And you knew all along?"

"Yes."

"I looked just like her at that age. I could see it instantly when they walked in. It was odd. Almost like looking in a mirror to the past but... different."

"Are you mad at me?"

"I'm not happy with you, but I'll be okay. We'll be okay." She waved her hands in the space between us. "I just can't believe you didn't tell me, especially after all we have been through recently."

"Mandy, I've been screwed up for years, most of my life. I'm only now getting myself together. And then here he comes back to town. We've been reconnecting, and it felt so good, and I kept telling myself I would find the right moment. I was going to tell you. I really was, but... Well, I didn't expect it to play out like this. I thought I would get to tell him first, in private, when I could explain."

"I understand. I think. I love you, Mama." She leaned over and hugged me. "I better head home with the kids. Don't worry. It will all work out. I don't know him, but I think he will forgive you too."

"You are just like him, you know."

She smiled at me. I think she liked hearing me say that, and then she was gone. I turned to Mary, embarrassed by all that transpired.

"Mary, I'm so sorry about the drama. I understand if you want to let me go."

"Are you kidding me?" She laughed. "I just had one of my best days ever. You, my dear, are never leaving. And that little drama? That's nothing. Try having a gay son! He is always high drama."

As she walked into the kitchen, she was chuckling and then started singing about money. Her happiness put a smile on my face.

I couldn't tell if she was kidding about Sean or not. I really don't remember him being overly dramatic. He was popular, always smiling, and borderline class clown, the type that brought comic relief. Maybe that is what she was doing now.

Well, the secret was out now.

Not the way I would have wanted it, and I knew it was far from over, but at least they knew. Lisa had told me to control the narrative. Instead, I had let it explode in a public bakery with our children watching.

Mandy would handle it better, I was sure. Ricky was another story. Not only him, but he had to deal with Amelia, who was clearly upset.

I had one job. Tell him before today. And I couldn't even do that.

There was nothing I could do now. I would just have to deal with things as they came.

I took a deep breath, wiped my eyes, and got back to work. It was all I could do.

Chapter Seven

Yesterday had been crazy. I had to sit Missy and Davy down to explain about Mandy's father. I thought it would be better to tell them myself than hear it from Darla at school, and who knew what Ricky had told his kids.

"So, Darla's dad is Mandy's dad too?" Missy asked.

"Yes, that's right. I knew him years ago."

"And that's when you had Mandy?"

"Yes."

"But why didn't he know her?"

"Because I kept it a secret."

"That wasn't nice." She scolded.

When did she get so smart and grown up?

"I know, and I should have told him."

She nodded, looking at me with those big eyes. Even at almost five, she understood that what I had done was wrong. Out of the mouths of babes.

"Do you have any other questions?" I asked.

"Does this make Darla and I sisters?"

"No, just her and Mandy because they have the same dad."

"Um, okay." She leaned over and hugged me before running off to play.

Davy didn't ask any questions and just watched our whole exchange. When Missy ran off, he followed her.

Then I spent the rest of the evening making my quick bread for the bakery. It felt so good to have a purpose and a direction in life.

It felt even better to have my biggest secret out in the open. I knew it wasn't over, but just having it out there felt like a weight lifted. For eighteen years, I had carried that secret like a stone in my chest. Now it was gone, and I could breathe a little easier. Even if the way it came out had been a disaster.

Mandy took the kids to daycare, so I headed to the bakery a bit earlier this morning. I got there and noticed that Ricky was standing outside.

My stomach dropped. What was he doing here?

After yesterday, I wouldn't have blamed him if he never wanted to see me again. But there he was, leaning against the brick wall next to the door, two coffees in his hands.

I sat in my car for a moment, gripping the steering wheel. I could do this. I had faced worse. I had faced the accident, the hospital, the withdrawal, the shame of looking my daughter in the eye and admitting I had failed her. I could face Ricky.

I squared my shoulders and got out of the car to face him. But first, I opened the back seat and started grabbing my baked goodies.

He saw me and started my way. He looked tired, like he hadn't slept much either. But he didn't look as angry as yesterday. That was something.

"Here, let me help you with those." He set the coffees on my car roof and took some of the bundles I had. Still a gentleman, even after everything. "Oh, and good morning. I brought you coffee. Figured you might need it after yesterday."

"Thanks, and good morning to you." I brushed a stray hair out of my face. "Ricky, I'm so sorry. About yesterday. About all of it. I should have told you at the coffee shop. I should have told you years ago. I just..."

"I know." He let out a long breath. "I'm still upset, Becca. I'm not going to pretend I'm not. You let me walk into that bakery without any warning. You sat across from me and talked about the past, and you never once mentioned that we had a daughter together."

"I know. I was wrong. I was scared."

"Scared of what? Of me?" He looked genuinely hurt by the thought.

"Scared of losing you again. Scared that once you knew the truth, you'd hate me. And I couldn't bear that. Not after we'd just found each other again."

He was quiet for a moment. "I don't hate you, Becca. I'm angry. I'm hurt. But I don't hate you."

"You should."

"Maybe. But that's not how I work." He handed me one of the coffees. "I spent all night thinking about it. About Mandy. About all the years I missed. And yeah, I'm furious that you kept her from me. But I also keep thinking about that scared fourteen-year-old girl who thought she was doing the right thing. Who thought she was protecting me."

Tears welled in my eyes. "I was trying to protect you. Your scholarship, your future. I didn't want to be the thing that held you back."

"I know. And that's the only reason I'm standing here right now instead of..." He trailed off, shaking his head. "I don't know what I would have done. Gone back to Austin, maybe. But that's not who I want to be. I don't want to be the guy who runs away from hard things."

"You were never that guy."

"Neither were you. You just got lost for a while." He looked at me, really looked at me. "I want to know her, Becca. I want to know my daughter."

"She wants to know you too."

"Yeah?" A small smile broke through. "What's she like? I mean, I saw her yesterday, but we didn't exactly get to talk."

"She's incredible. She's kind and hardworking and so much stronger than I ever was. She raised her siblings while I was too drunk to function. She built a business from nothing. She's..." I choked up. "She's the best parts of both of us, Ricky. And none of the worst parts of me."

"I'd like to find that out for myself. Can I call you sometime? To set something up?"

"Of course. Yeah." My face warmed, and despite everything, butterflies flitted around in my stomach. This wasn't how I'd imagined any of this going, but here we were. "I'd like that."

"Good." He shifted the bundles in his arms. "Now let's get these inside before Mary thinks you're slacking on day two."

Mary opened the door for us so we could bring in the cakes. We then went back for the second load.

"I would like to officially meet her. How does she feel about this? Do you think she would be open to meeting me?" He asked as we arranged the loaves.

"Yes, yes, she would be. She was upset at first too, but we talked a lot last night. I pretty much told her everything, as well as my younger two. I wanted them to hear it from me and not Darla or someone else. You know?"

"Makes sense. Amelia did get Darla all worked up. But once she was calm, Darla was happy about Mandy being her sister. I guess she had met her at the daycare and likes her a lot. She also thinks it makes her and Missy sisters. I tried to explain, but she is five." He shrugged.

I laughed. "Missy said the same thing. I had to explain to her that's not how it works."

"They'll figure it out eventually." He paused at the door. "So, I'll call you? To set up a time for me to meet Mandy properly?"

"Please."

He bought a few slices of banana bread before leaving. At the door, he turned back.

"Becca? I'm glad you're doing better. I really am. And I'm glad I'm here to see it."

Then he was gone.

"Well, well, well, Ms. Becca. Off to a better start than yesterday." Mary smirked at me from behind the counter.

I just smiled and then started slicing the rest of the bread and loading them into the case.

Thankfully, the rest of my day wasn't eventful, other than selling out of my bread and having to make more again. Mary was thrilled.

"I should have hired you years ago." She said. "I swear over half of Glenn Lake has been in the shop the past two days."

"It seems like it." I beamed.

One of the employees named Jade said, "This has been a huge hit. I'm so jealous."

"Oh, Jade, your cookies are excellent."

"Yeah, but they are all Mary's recipes. Not mine."

I smiled and helped the next customers that just walked in.

This was exactly what I needed in my life. A purpose, direction, something to be proud of. Not that I wasn't proud of my children, but I had never known how to be a mother.

Baking was easy. It was fun, and if you made a mistake, you threw it in the trash and started over. You couldn't throw away the years you lost with your kids and start fresh. You just had to keep going and hope the next batch turned out better.

When I got home at the end of the day, I was exhausted. The good kind of exhausted.

I collapsed on the couch and didn't move for about ten minutes. I might have let myself doze off if it wasn't for the fact I would need to start dinner.

I pushed myself up with a grunt as my body protested. It was not used to the physical work of standing and moving all day.

"We aren't done yet," I whispered to myself as I pulled out a cutting board to start making dinner.

It was nearly done cooking when I heard the kids come through the front door. I turned from the sink, drying my hands as I went to go meet them.

"Hey, y'all. How was school?" I asked as I joined them in the living room.

"It was great. I played with Darla, and we talked about Mandy a lot." She looked up at her big sister with a smile. "She wanted to know everything about you."

"What did you tell her?" Mandy asked.

"I said your favorite color is green, but I couldn't remember your birthday. You love banana bread." Missy looked at me. "And you are the best sister ever."

"Aw, that's sweet, but I think you're the best sister ever." She winked at her little sister.

"I am a good one," Missy said.

"I good too," Davy added.

"Of course you are, but you're a brother."

"Oh!"

"Dinner is almost ready." I said. "Go wash up."

The little kids bounced down the hallway to the bathroom. Mandy followed me into the kitchen.

"How was the second day of work? Any more secrets to share?" She teased.

"Yeah, I'm actually an alien from outer space."

"Ha, ha. But seriously, how was today?"

"Great. We sold out of everything again. Mary was happy."

"I bet."

"Ricky... er... your dad came by to talk to me." I said, wincing a little at the awkward way it felt saying the word dad.

"Oh, how did that go?" If she felt uncomfortable with the new title, she didn't say or give any indication.

"Better than I expected. He was still upset, but... he wants to know you, Mandy. He asked if you'd be open to meeting him. Properly this time."

"I'd like that." She smiled at me, and there was something soft in her eyes. Hope, maybe. The same hope I was feeling.

"I thought you would."

I watched her walk to the table to set it for dinner. My daughter. His daughter. After eighteen years of secrets, they would finally know each other.

I didn't know what would come next. But for the first time in a long time, I wasn't dreading the future. I was curious about it.

Chapter Eight

I worked through the weekend, and then I had a few days off to take care of my counseling, doctor's appointments, and meet with the district attorney in the case against Butch.

His trial would be soon, and they wanted to discuss my part as a witness with me prior. Chances were good he was going to jail for the rest of his life. I could only hope, because he scared me. He had pure evil in his eyes and heart.

When we were still dating, he would drink himself stupid and fly into these fits of rage. It was kind of like what I would do to Mandy. I didn't connect that in my mind until after the accident, and I started my counseling sessions.

I apologized to her more than once. Being a saint, she accepted without much fanfare and, in fact, kind of blew it off as no big deal. My therapist had suggested it could be her way of coping with it. Ignore, block, and pretend it was no big deal. Either way, what the heck did I do to deserve that girl? I would work the rest of my life to make that up to her.

The night of the accident, I had finally gotten up the nerve to break up with him. I thought if I did it in a public place, he couldn't hurt me.

As I expected, he did not take it well and drank all day, which I should have known would make him unpredictable. I had been drinking for my courage and probably wasn't thinking clearly. He forced me out of the bar. I was careful not to make a scene as I didn't want to get arrested for public intoxication. I knew he could lie with the best of them, and somehow it would be my fault.

Once we were away from others, he grabbed my neck and held me a few inches off the ground, slamming my back and head against the brick wall. I saw stars instantly. He hit me a few more times for good measure before dropping me, and when I tried to plead with him, he backhanded me across the face. I was barely conscious. That is when he dragged me to the car.

As we made our way through the parking lot towards his car, a few people noticed us. He explained I had had a little too much to drink. I tried to speak, but I couldn't form words, and the sounds came out as slurred nonsense.

In my head, I was screaming for help, begging for my life. I didn't want to get in the car with him. A nightmare was waiting for me. If we made it home, there would be no witnesses.

I don't remember much about that drive, but I know he was yelling insults at me, graphically describing what he planned to do when we got home.

He didn't need to tell me because I already knew what happened behind closed doors. He would unleash all kinds of nightmarish abuse.

I must have had a guardian angel of sorts watching out for me because, thankfully, we never made it home. I felt horrible for the family in the other car. Beyond awful. But for me, it probably saved my life. I now have a second chance to make it up to my children and to myself.

All things I was working through in therapy. I couldn't wait to give Lisa an update on the job. Though I was dreading telling her the story of how the secret got out. She had wanted me to tell them myself so that it didn't happen this way. She said it was essential for my growth and facing my fears. I knew I would cry a lot before the appointment ended.

"So, Becca, last week we talked about you telling Mandy and Ricky the truth before your first day. How did that go?"

I took a deep breath. "Well, actually, it didn't go the way any of us planned."

I described the scene at the bakery. How Ricky had walked in with his kids. How I had frozen. How everything unraveled in front of everyone. She took notes, asked questions, and took more notes.

"I know I don't need to say it, but that is why we were going to have a plan." She said, putting her pen down. "So, what are the next steps?"

"Ricky came back the next day. We talked. He was hurt, and rightfully so. But he's... he's being incredibly gracious about it. More than I deserve." I twisted the tissue in my hands. "He's asked to meet Mandy, to get to know her. She's excited to get to know him too. Even though she never really asked about her father growing up, I know she's been curious. I think she just listened to the rumors around town about who he was or wasn't. Ricky was seldom mentioned in those stories."

"And why was that?"

"Because my parents were powerful and told people what they wanted them to believe. It wasn't a secret that Ricky and I were dating, though."

"Tell me again why you didn't tell him about the baby?"

"He had a college scholarship. He would be the first in his family to go." I looked down at my lap. "I couldn't take that away from him, and I thought my parents would take care of us. I was just a young child myself."

She nodded and made notes. We then continued with my appointment, discussing my progress and how I needed to keep focusing on my goals with the kids.

By the end of this, I felt the need for a strong drink or a nap, or both. But I wasn't going to give in, at least to the alcohol. It sucked. Would always feel this way. All I could do was continue to move forward, keep repeating my goals, focus on my kids, and work at Mary's.

Next up for my day was the meeting with the district attorney. I knew this was going to be emotional and draining as well. There were several people involved, from the DA, an assistant, and a few police officers.

They wanted me to recount the events of that night. I could almost feel it all happening again as I spoke. The fear. The helplessness. His hands around my throat. I held my composure and tried to be calm, though my heart was pounding in my ears. I got through it somehow, and when it ended, I practically ran to my car.

I was spent. Emotionally drained. The stress made my body ache, and I wanted to fall apart. I definitely wanted that drink and a nap.

However, my new life and goals meant I had to suck it up, refocus, and pull myself together. That was what all this hard work was about, after all.

One bright spot in my day was when I had dropped off several dozen pans of homemade goodies at Mary's this morning. I made several batches of them each night to deliver to her each morning, whether I was working or not.

They had quickly become her most popular items, and of course, Mary loved the increase in business and praised me endlessly.

She also gave Rich Donovan free coffee when he would come in as a thank you for the suggestion. He came in nearly every day and was typically our first customer.

Each day it was more or less the same routine.

"Best banana bread I have had. And my Mama used to make the best, God rest her soul, but it was nothing like this. Mm-mmm." He bought half a loaf, got his free coffee to go, and wished us well.

We brainstormed some new recipes. However, I needed to practice them a little more before bringing them into the store. For example, I didn't have the double chocolate chip banana bread quite where I wanted it yet, but close.

So, before introducing them at the store, I wanted them to be perfect as I didn't want to let Mary down. She was amazing to give me a chance, and I didn't want to blow it.

When I got home from the district attorney's office, Mandy was pulling in with the kids. That got my mind refocused and ended my pity party. I hated all my alone time, and my babies would put a smile on my face.

"Hi Mama, how was your day?" Mandy asked, leaning forward to hug me. I needed that.

"Um, boring, long, emotional. They asked a lot of questions. I'm not looking forward to this trial. How about you?" I hugged the little kids as they hopped out of the car and ran to me.

"Ricky called me." She had told me I could give him her number, so I did.

"Oh yeah? How did that go?"

"We are going to meet for lunch tomorrow. I'm nervous but also excited." She giggled.

"I'm sure it will go well."

On my own with the little kids that night, it was the second bright spot of my day. Mandy and Jimmy were going on a double date with his friend Ty and his latest girlfriend.

Poor guy seemed to have a new girlfriend every week, but I didn't get the impression he was a playboy or anything. I had met Ty a few times, and he seemed nice. I guess, like me, he hadn't found what or who he was looking for.

I decided to make us a homemade pizza.

"Who's gonna help me?" I asked the kids.

"Oh, me! Me!" they both yelled, jumping around.

We mixed up the dough, and then I let them take turns trying to roll it out.

"This is fun, Mama," Missy said.

"So fun. So fun." Davy agreed.

"Oh, this looks so good. Okay, next, toppings."

"I love this pepperoni," Missy said, spreading them out.

Davy, on the other hand, put them all in the same spot. I grinned and helped get them spread out more. As the final step, we added some vegetables and cheese.

"It looks great. Are we ready to cook it?"

"Yeah!"

I slid it in the oven and set the timer. We cleaned up while it cooked.

The stress melted away with each smile, each laugh. The spontaneous hugs and kisses from my babies made everything better. How had I lived so long without this?

"We should eat this in the living room like a picnic and watch a movie. What do you guys think?"

"Oh, yes, please, can we? Can we?" Missy clapped.

"Movie, pizza, movie!" Davy bounced around as he sang his request.

They ran into the living room to pick out a movie. I just smiled as I listened to them discussing it. They settled on Finding Nemo. Always a good choice and a favorite of mine.

Once the pizza was ready, I sliced it up and put two slices on a plate for each of us. We got settled around the coffee table facing the TV. The kids had the hugest smiles as they happily ate pizza and watched the movie. We had all seen the movie so often that we could quote most of it, and we did.

When the movie was over and the pizza was eaten, I gave them baths, read to them, and kissed them good night.

"Mama?"

"Yes, sweetie?"

"This was the most fun ever. Thanks for the pizza picnic and the movie." Missy leaned forward to hug me.

"Tank you, Mama," Davy said, following his sister's lead.

"I enjoyed it too. We will have to do it again very soon."

I kissed them both once more and went to finish cleaning the kitchen so I could start on my baking for the next day. I was behind a little bit, but it was worth it.

Thankfully, Mary had let me borrow several loaf pans so I could have a bunch going at once. It took time, but I finally had them all made and everything cleaned up.

It was a little late, but I wasn't tired yet, so I roamed around the house looking for something to do. I picked up a few stray items, started some laundry, and folded a load of towels.

Once those were put away, I settled in front of the television. I flipped through the guide to find something to watch, deciding on the Food Network. My favorite.

My phone notification chimed. I peeked, and my pulse quickened. It was from Ricky. It was just a simple hi, but it made me smile. I replied. Then my phone rang.

"Hey, Ricky."

"Hello. Sorry, I know it's late, but I thought I would just call to say hi and let you know... I was thinking about you."

"That's so sweet. I was thinking about you too, actually."

"I'm meeting Mandy tomorrow. Did she tell you?"

"She did."

"I'm nervous. I don't know what to say to her."

"Nothing special. Just get to know her. I think you will love her."

"I already do, and I only had a five minute conversation with her. I can't wait to get to know her more."

My heart fluttered. He was a good man. So why did I break his heart? Why did I keep his daughter from him?

We chatted about nothing and everything. Old memories. Whatever happened to so and so. Our kids, especially Darla and Missy's instant friendship.

"The girls were instant friends. Darla is all Missy talks about."

"I'm so happy for Darla that she found friends. She's had a lot of change."

"Yes, I'm happy for them. They have such an adorable friendship, though I had heard from Mandy that Olive isn't happy about it. She's feeling left out a bit."

"I'll talk to Darla."

"Good. I've already talked to Missy too."

"Would it be wrong if I asked you out?" Ricky asked.

My heart nearly stopped. "I think it would be okay." I tried to say it calmly, but in my mind, I was yelling, Heck, yes!

"How about dinner tomorrow night?"

"Yes, that would be fun." I couldn't stop smiling.

After discussing the details, we said good night. I jumped up and danced around the living room. I was so into my celebratory dance that I didn't notice the front door open.

"Having a good evening, Mama?"

"Oh! That's a bit embarrassing." I sat quickly on the couch.

"It's just me." She laughed. "So, what's that happy dance for?"

"I just hung up with Ricky. Your dad." That sounded odd and good to say. "He asked me out to dinner." I giggled a little.

"Oh, Mama, that's so cute. You still like him." She paused and got a serious look on her face. "You really loved him, didn't you?"

"Oh, baby, I still do. I have always loved him."

I had tears in my eyes, but they were happy tears. She walked over and wrapped me in her arms. I pulled her into my lap. She was a good foot taller than me, but she was still my baby. It felt a little foreign but oh so wonderful to just hold her and sit like this.

We sat like that, talking about our evening. I told her about our pizza picnic, and she talked about the movie she saw with Jimmy. We both shared about work. It was nice to have a normal conversation.

"Well, I hope it works out for you. I really do. Not because he is my father, but because I can tell he makes you happy."

She kissed my cheek and then stood. We said good nights, and then she went to her room.

I turned off the TV, checked that my cakes were all wrapped up, and went to bed myself. I actually slept without guilt, without bad thoughts or nightmares. It was a pleasant change.

Chapter Nine

The next day I went into work loaded with tons of cakes for Mary. She was overjoyed.

"I missed you here the past few days. I ran out quickly. Huge, huge hit." She gestured wildly. "I think this will be a huge draw because they won't always be available. Like my snickerdoodles."

Even though I baked for her each night before my days off, I wasn't there to bake more during the day.

"Personally, I love the oatmeal cookies the best."

She just grinned at my comment.

We had a busy day. I was beat by the time we closed. I could use a soak in the tub and a nap, but I had to rush to get ready for my date. I didn't want to smell like baked goods. Well, I guess there were worse things to smell like, but clean was definitely better.

After I was showered and dressed, the kids were just getting home. It was Jimmy's turn to pick them up. Our custody arrangement seemed to work well for everyone. They mostly slept at my house, but he still saw them nearly every day. Much better than when I was selfish and ran him off.

Shortly after Jimmy and the kids arrived, Mandy made it home. Jimmy was having dinner here tonight, as he did a few times a week. I don't know many people who see their exes quite as much as I see mine.

At first, it was a little strange. Not just him dating Mandy but just having him around again. Things with us hadn't ended well, which was my fault. Seeing him reminded me how awful I had been.

"Oh, Mama, you look so pretty." Little Davy was super sweet.

"Yes, you look very nice. Are you excited?" Mandy asked.

"Yes, and a little nervous. Did you have a nice time at lunch?"

"Yeah. It was slightly awkward at first, but we have a lot in common. Did you know he is a math teacher? He loves math like I do." The excitement in her voice was unmistakable. It made me both happy and sad.

"He was always good at math. He used to help me with my homework. He had this way of explaining it that actually made sense to me. So maybe that is why I like math too."

"He told me I could call him dad. I think I will get used to it, but it seems a little strange right now."

"Oh, that's awesome. I'm sure you'll get used to it."

She smiled. "Well, have fun tonight." She headed to the kitchen to start their dinner. I waited near the front door.

I paced and peeked through the blinds every few seconds, waiting on him. The butterflies in my stomach were working double time right now. I checked my purse to make sure I had everything I needed. Keys, phone, wallet. All good. Anything to keep my mind off of waiting.

When I saw his car come around the corner and stop in front of my house, the butterflies kicked it up a notch. He knocked, and I counted to ten. Okay, five. Before opening it.

"Hey, you look... wow, great." My cheeks warmed as he let his eyes look me up and down.

"Hi, Ricky. You look great yourself."

"Are you ready?"

"Sure." I yelled to Mandy, and she came into the living room to say hi.

It was weird hearing her say dad. That was never a word we really used during her life. Not about my dad, not about hers.

"Well, y'all have fun." She said as we headed out.

He opened the car door for me. He'd done that in high school too. What teenage boy did that? I'd had something wonderful, and I let it go.

"Is the temperature okay? Not too hot?" It was Texas. It was always hot.

"Nope, I'm comfortable. Thanks."

He had the radio on the 90s channel. It was like a flashback to high school. We sang along with a few favorites and talked about memories that went with a few others. A school dance, a pep rally, or a scene from a favorite movie. It made what could have been an awkward drive fun and comforting.

We headed to Pearland for dinner. It was a larger town and had more options for dining. We ended up at a new family owned Italian restaurant. I had heard rave reviews about it.

We ordered stuffed mushrooms and calamari, making small talk while we waited. We talked about work, people in town, and our kids. Safe topics, but not how we felt about each other or feelings in general. Whatever he was thinking, I didn't want to go there. Not yet. At least not yet.

At some point in there, the appetizers arrived.

"So, you're a math teacher now. You were always great at math."

"Yeah, I got to college and started out in computer science, but after my freshman year, I just decided to switch. I love teaching."

"I think that is great." I stabbed a piece of mushroom.

"Thanks. I enjoy it a lot. I can't wait to be teaching at the old high school." He squeezed lemon over the calamari then helped himself to a few pieces.

"Mandy said you had a nice lunch. How do you think it went?"

"It was nice. Though a little weird because I kept thinking, wow, I have an adult daughter. But I enjoyed it a lot. She seems great."

"She is. I am so proud of how she's turned out, despite my lack of... Well, I wasn't the best, but she is wonderful. Caring. Hardworking."

I didn't want to keep apologizing to him for keeping her from him, so I left that part out even though it was on the tip of my tongue. I also didn't want to mention my lack of mothering. Everyone knew that. He didn't even know about her, but I was sure he had already heard what a wreck I had been through the Glenn Lake grapevine.

"I can't believe she runs her own business. That is incredible."

"Yeah, she started it at age twelve, I think. She is amazing. Already has a few employees. Pays bills, taxes, including business taxes. What kid thinks of those things? I'm an adult, and I wouldn't have thought of that right away."

"I'm looking forward to getting to know her better. We are planning to get together for lunch again next week. Make it a regular thing."

Our entrees arrived shortly after, and we focused a little more on eating, chatting here and there. To some, it might seem uncomfortable to sit and not talk, but for us, it was comfortable. It was as if those nineteen years melted away, and we were just us again.

I kept looking at him and still couldn't believe I was on a date with Ricky Torres after all this time. I almost felt like my fourteen year old self again. I had been so proud to be his girlfriend back then. If we ended up dating again, I would be just as proud today too.

He was quiet on the drive home. I wasn't sure if that was a good thing or not. I wished I knew what he was thinking. Was he thinking about us? Was he thinking about his kids? Or was he just thinking guy stuff like beer, fishing, and football?

We pulled up in front of my house. He put the car in park and then turned to face me. "Well, here we are."

"Yes, here we are."

"So, um, I'll be honest with you." He exhaled. "I'm not sure what I want or what I can give you in the way of a relationship at this point. I'm still in love with my wife. She has only been gone for about a year now." He paused, but I didn't say a word. My heart was crushed. "But I do want to see you again. I just want to let you know that I'm still healing. I don't want to seem like I'm leading you on or anything."

He took my hand. We just sat there for a moment, looking at each other.

"I understand. I think."

"I just don't have much of myself to give to a relationship right now. A friendship? Yes. But not a romantic relationship. Plus, I am still trying to process having another child. I have three young children to care for, and we have only just moved back to the area. We have so much going on right now. Amelia is not doing well with all the change and especially the idea of me dating."

I was having a hard time understanding what he was saying. Then he leaned over and kissed me gently on the lips. It was so simple, but oh, so wonderful. I always thought actions spoke louder than words, which made this that much more puzzling.

He sat back in his seat and smiled. "I have thought about you over the years, and I did miss you."

"I missed you too." My heart ached. In ways, this felt like a breakup and oddly like we were getting back together.

"Well, as much as I hate to say it, I need to say good night because I have to get my kids from Maria and Carl's. I had a great time tonight."

"I did too."

He walked me to the door, giving me another quick kiss. "I'll text you tomorrow. Good night."

"Good night." I smiled, unlocked the door, and went in.

Once safely behind the door, I peeked through a slit in the blinds. He got in his car and drove off.

When I couldn't see his car any longer, I let out a sigh and a few tears. I didn't understand what he meant. He liked me but couldn't commit to a relationship right now.

He said he wanted to continue to see me. That gave me hope that something could be rekindled between us. Then there were the soft, sweet kisses. I just kept thinking actions speak louder than words. He was healing and maybe was as confused as me.

I slid down the door to the floor. I sat there with my head in my hands, head spinning from all the thoughts and feelings. I hated my feelings. God, I wanted a drink right now to dull the hurt, the confusion, but I wouldn't. Instead, I focused on my children. I counted to ten and repeated each of their names.

I continued to sit there for a while, trying to clear my head of everything but my children's faces. I was thankful Mandy wasn't at the computer working. She must be in in her room, so I just focused on breathing again.

After several minutes of that, I felt a lot better. I wouldn't fall off the wagon tonight. So, with a few hours of baking to do, I stood up and headed to the kitchen. That would definitely refocus my mind on something else.

"Oh, Mama, I thought I heard you come in. How was dinner?" Mandy came into the kitchen.

I hoped she didn't notice I had been crying.

"It was nice. I had chicken parm. My fave."

"Yummy. And you had a nice time?"

"Yes, I did. Nothing serious, but just a nice dinner as friends." I tried to smile.

I think I did. If she saw through my charade of faking my happiness, she didn't comment. Instead, she wished me a good night.

"Do you need help baking?"

"Sure, that would be nice."

We got right to work. Measuring and mixing. Pouring and baking. As we worked, my phone chirped that I received a text. It was from Ricky. A smile spread on my face.

Good night, beautiful

Good night, handsome

"Was that dad?"

"Yes." My pulse quickened at the thought of him.

"You are blushing. How cute!"

I felt my cheeks and grinned at her. So help me, I was still in love with this man, but I had no idea what I would do. It was a confusing situation, and the only thing I understood about it was I wanted this in whatever shape or form he was willing to give.

"Yes, well..." I shrugged, and we got back to work.

Soon we finished all the cakes for the next day. We wrapped them up and got them packaged for the morning. I thanked her for helping me, and we said good night. It had been a good night for sure.

Confusing, but good.

Chapter Ten

The rest of the week was fairly uneventful, with work four days in a row. I was still experimenting with recipes. Today I brought in banana bread, brown sugar pound cake, and lemon blueberry pound cake.

Mary went gaga for them.

"I'm a genius for hiring you. Best decision." She high fived me.

I was over the moon with pride at all her praise. I had never gotten this kind of positive attention before. It felt amazing, and no matter how many times she told me, it felt as good as the first time.

All my life, I have tried to feel loved, accepted, and get this positive feedback. When that hadn't worked, I had let myself spiral helplessly and hopelessly out of control or found comfort in the arms of any man that would have me. Unfortunately, it was usually the abusive type.

For the first time, things were going well, and I was trying not to do the classic Becca thing by blowing it.

"I'm not that Becca anymore," I said to myself and continued stocking the display case.

A group of tourists came in, so I stood with a smile.

"Welcome to Mary's Bakery. How can I help you?" I greeted.

"We heard about some good banana bread. Is that here?" The father asked.

"Yes, it is," I said proudly.

I got their order together and thanked them for coming in. As they left, another family came in, and then a few ladies came in. This was how it was each and every day. I loved this job.

As I worked, I thought of Ricky. We talked each day either on the phone or via text. He would start out with a text to tell me good morning and always end the day with a good night. Each one made me smile, blush, or giggle like a schoolgirl.

He had been my biggest crush, my first and only love. I had dated a lot of men since or had random hookups with guys so they would pay for things for me, but I had never loved anyone else.

I couldn't believe that he was back in my life. It didn't feel real. Though I still didn't know where things stood, and he hadn't said either way, not since our dinner date.

I'm sure we'd talk about it soon, but until then, all I could do was guess and stress about how his words didn't match his actions. What did it mean?

Finally, on my day off, Ricky and I were meeting for a lunch date at his family's restaurant. I hadn't been to Abuelita Carmen's for years. I used to almost live there when we were dating.

I was nervous about facing his family. How had they taken the news about Mandy? Would they hate me or accept me? I used to be almost a member of the family and then a sudden stranger.

When we had broken up, I had mourned losing his family's love almost as much as losing him.

When I stepped inside, it was like going back in time. The interior had not changed. Everything from the red leather booths, the jewel colored carpet, and the delicious smells wafting from the kitchen was almost like coming home, but what would the reception be? It took all of two seconds to find out.

"Becca! Oh, it is wonderful to see you again, mija." His mom pulled me in for a hug. I guess they weren't mad.

"Hi, Mrs. Torres. It's great to see you too."

"Oh, please call me Rosa. You're a grown woman now."

"Okay, thanks, Rosa."

"Ricky's in the back. You remember the way, yes?"

She gestured towards the kitchen and then greeted the next patrons that came in. I didn't take the abrupt dismissal as a negative. I understood that it was lunch, and the restaurant was always busy.

I walked through the restaurant to the kitchen with several sets of eyes on me. Some were just nosy customers, but a few were his family members that worked in the restaurant.

His cousin Loretta called out to me as she walked by with a tray of drinks. "Hey, Becca, how are you?"

"Hey, Loretta. Good. Good to see you." I kept walking. I just wanted to get to Ricky and away from the main dining area, or at least to his side, so I didn't feel so on display.

I knew the kitchen like the back of my hand. I had spent a lot of time at the restaurant once upon a time. It was almost like a second home as Ricky worked a lot, and I liked spending time with him. I noticed him immediately doing dishes like he always did. He said it relaxed him.

He looked up and caught me staring. Not the first or last time I had done that. I couldn't help but smile at the thought and at him.

"Becca, hey. I didn't know you were here already." He grabbed a towel to dry his hands. Then he leaned over and kissed my cheek. "You look beautiful today."

"Thanks, Ricky."

"Are you ready to eat? I reserved us a table." I nodded.

As we walked back through the kitchen to the main dining area, his grandma Carmen smiled and blew me a kiss as we walked by. I loved his family, and it looked like they still loved me. Why had I stayed away from them for so long? Why had I thought not including them would be best for all of us? We all missed out over the past eighteen years. I just didn't realize it until this moment. They didn't know Mandy. She didn't know what a wonderful, loving family she had. And they didn't know her. I mentally kicked myself for like the millionth time.

We sat in the back corner near the windows overlooking Glenn Lake Park. It was gorgeous today, and there were several people outside enjoying it. I imagined there would be a few moms with young kids letting them play on the playground, people walking dogs or throwing a ball for them, and others walking the trails alone or maybe standing out on the pier watching the ripples in the water. Tourists and locals alike enjoyed the park. It was one of the reasons people came to Glenn Lake.

His cousin Martin was our waiter. He came with chips and salsa and then took our order of fajitas for two. I was looking forward to Carmen's tortillas.

"So, Darla is excited about Missy's party this weekend. It is all she is talking about."

"Missy is excited too. She invited her whole class, and I think almost every one of them is coming."

"The weather sounds a little iffy, though."

"Yeah, I'm a little worried but hoping it will be okay. It was my main concern when she said she wanted it at the park."

"I bet."

We continued to chat about the party, then changed topics to kids in general. He was making plans for them for the summer. Then we shifted topics to baseball, not that I was all that interested, but the season had just gotten started, and it was looking good for the home team. I had forgotten how much of a baseball fan he was, but not nearly as big of a fan as he was of football. Football season would be crazy.

Martin checked on us a few times, refilling our drinks, bringing our food, and visiting with us when he heard us talking about baseball. Loretta stopped by once, as well as a few of his other cousins. His brother Manny came from the kitchen after our dinner was delivered.

"Hey, Becca! What are you doing seeing this loser again?" His voice boomed. He sat next to me and gave me a hug.

"Oh, you know me, Manny. I'm a sucker for the underdog." I grinned at Ricky, and he just winked in reply.

"How is your food? Still as good as always, right?"

"Of course."

"So why have you stayed away so long? We have missed you."

"Shut up, Manny. She doesn't have to explain herself." Ricky punched him in the arm.

"Hey, we're all thinking it. I just have the balls to ask. But that's fine. She doesn't have to answer. I know it was because you weren't here." He punched Ricky back, winked at me, and then walked back to the kitchen, stopping at tables to ask how things were or waving to other customers as he went by.

"I'm sorry for him. He's an idiot."

"No, no, it's fine. I remember how he is."

"I hope that he doesn't change your mind about seeing me again." He looked at me hopefully.

"He couldn't change my mind that easily."

"Good."

We finished up our meals. He left a tip for Martin. Loretta and Rosa both hugged me as I was leaving.

"Now, don't you be a stranger, Becca. And please bring those kiddos around to meet us, especially that Mandy." Were those tears in Rosa's eyes? She hadn't gotten to meet her granddaughter yet, so perhaps.

"I'll bring them soon. I promise, and we'll see you for Missy's party?"

"I wouldn't miss it for the world."

Out on the street, he suggested a walk in the park. We walked towards the lake and around the east side towards one of the elevated decks. We stood over the water watching the ducks. He moved towards me and put an arm around my waist, pulling me a little closer to his side.

We didn't say anything. It didn't feel like words were needed. We were together, and that was what mattered. After several minutes, he turned me to him. The look in his eyes made me swoon. He was going to kiss me. It was just a soft, simple kiss, but I melted. It ended too quickly for me. Then again, I never wanted it to end, so any length of time wouldn't have been enough. I had waited too long for this moment.

"Are you ready to go?"

"Sure." Though I wanted to yell no.

He took my hand, and we walked back to the parking lot near the restaurant. He stopped at my car, brushed back a piece of hair behind my ear, and kissed me again. Goosebumps head to toe.

"I'll call you later. Thanks for meeting me for lunch."

"Thank you for lunch. Talk to you later." I drove away on cloud nine.

Chapter Eleven

I sat nervously in the parking lot in front of the civic center. Today I was going to a group therapy session, and I wasn't looking forward to it. My counselor said I only had to share if I wanted to, but I was still uneasy about this.

Checking the clock, I was early by about fifteen minutes. Too soon to go in, but the right amount of time to sit here fretting over how this meeting would go.

I turned the radio volume up a few notches as I watched a few cars pull in the lot, parking, but the occupants stayed in their vehicles. I guess we were all nervous.

Pulling out my cell phone, I opened a game that I liked to play. It was a good time waster. Then, finally, people started to get out of their cars to head in.

"Well, here goes nothing." I sighed.

I shut off my phone, grabbed my purse and my courage, and followed the others in. I smiled at a few that looked at me.

We walked down the quiet hallway, our footsteps echoing in the empty building. Several doors down was the meeting room. The room was set up with several pods of tables and chairs around them. The speaker was at the front by a podium.

We all took seats. Some people greeted each other with hellos and hugs. Others looked a little unsure, like me. I took a seat to the right of the podium with two other ladies.

"Welcome, everyone. Please take a seat. We'll be starting soon." The man at the podium said.

He was tall and thin, wearing a blazer over an old rock concert shirt. He smiled and greeted a few people that sat close to where he stood.

I watched as people settled, and a lady came in with a stack of papers. She started passing them out to everyone, along with a pen.

"Here you go. Mike will let you know what to do with it when it's time." She smiled warmly as she handed the packets to our table.

"Alright, I think we're ready to start. For those that are new, I'm Mike, and my partner is April." Mike turned to her.

"Hello, all." April waved.

"Tonight, we are here to dive into coping techniques for stress and how we can manage our disappointments."

He launched into a presentation about stress management. Eat healthier, get enough sleep, and exercise regularly were some of them that I felt I could do better at and control. Others like having a positive attitude, asserting myself, and focusing on things I could control seemed more overwhelming but doable.

"Would anyone like to share a time they felt overwhelmed, and what did you do to feel better? Or if you didn't control it, how was the experience?" Mike asked.

A few nervous laughs as people looked around to see who would volunteer first.

"Nobody?" April said.

"I'll go." A guy a table over from me stood. "It was after my wife left me, taking the kids and my dog. That was my dog before she and I got married. Anyway, I felt like life was just collapsing in on me. I made a lot of bad decisions, but thanks to joining this group, though court ordered, I channeled my anger and stress into positive. As a result, I now have my family back. Well, at least my kids." He smiled around at each person and then took a seat.

"That's good, Bruce. So, joining a group helped you. That's a good point and why you are all here." He started talking about how social support and meetings can help your mental health. "As people, we seek friendships and companions. We don't like to be alone."

Strange how alone I always felt, even when I was in a room full of people. I was missing significant connections in my life, like my parents. Both gone, but we never had a strong bond. I didn't have siblings or cousins. No grandparents.

I now had my own children, but I wasn't married, never have been. My children and I hadn't had much of a relationship until recently, so it was a new connection, I supposed.

I did have Stephanie. My oldest and dearest friend. Then a handful of neighbors that, despite everything I had done, still stood by me. And now I had Rachel, my sponsor, who answered the phone no matter what time I called.

My circle was small, but those that stayed with me had my back completely. Yet, even after counting my blessings, there were so many moments that I felt so very alone.

I started listening again as Mike began talking about the next technique.

"Having hobbies or special interests is another great way to relax and control stress. Who has a hobby or an interest they would like to share?"

Hands went up around the room. I guess this was an easier topic for people to talk about.

"I love needlepoint. I make all kinds of things. Pillows, wall hangings, ornaments." A lady at my table shared.

"I enjoy hiking." Someone else shared.

I didn't speak up, but I thought about baking. It might now be my job, but it was also therapeutic. It was creative yet precise. If the measurements weren't accurate, the final product would bomb.

I felt my hand go up, and to my horror, Mike called on me.

"Yes, Becca?" He said with a smile.

"I bake." I looked around. "I actually work in a bakery, and it has been a great outlet for me."

"Nice."

Others around me smiled, and then the meeting continued. I had done it. I shared during the group meeting. Something I had not planned to do, but I couldn't help it. When it came to my baking, I was proud.

The rest of the meeting went by in a flash. I felt like I had learned a few things from it and got a couple of new techniques. Maybe I would start exercising. It definitely couldn't hurt.

"Hey, Becca." April caught me before I left the meeting room.

"Yes?"

"I bake too. Where is the bakery? I'd love to stop by."

"Oh, it's in Glenn Lake. Mary's Bakery."

"I know that place. Nice. Her snickerdoodles are awesome. I always make it a point to come during December to get them."

"I make banana bread and other quick bread like that."

"How fun. It's fun to turn our hobbies into a job." She smiled. "Well, I'll see you next time, and I'll be sure to stop by the store to see you too."

"I look forward to it."

I felt so light as air as I left the civic center. The conversation with April was my favorite part. Finally, I had something to share with someone that wasn't just beer or a sad story.

I drove home, singing along with the radio and laughing at nothing but my pure happiness at being alive. It was a new feeling, and I liked it.

I got home in time to help with getting the little kids to bed.

"Yeah, Mama's home!" Missy cheered. "You can read with us."

"I'd love to."

We raced down the hall, laughing, and climbed into Missy's bed. She had the book already, so she opened it and started reading. Davy laid his head in my lap, and I stroked his hair.

We read two books, and by then, they were both yawning, ready for dreams. I kissed them both.

"Good night, babies," I said as I switched off their light and left.

"Wanna cup of tea?" Mandy asked when I walked into the kitchen.

"Yeah, thanks."

"So, how was the meeting?"

"It was good. They talked about how to deal with stress."

"Oh yeah?"

"Yeah. Hobbies are a good stress reliever, and I actually mentioned how I bake. I hadn't planned to speak, but it just happened." I grinned.

"That's great. What else?"

I told her about all the different things they talked about, including the exercise.

"And I thought I should find time to work out. Maybe going over to the park to walk, or even walking to work. I can put the bread in a wagon and walk to town."

"It's definitely walkable. I still walk a lot of days to my cleaning jobs." She set a hot cup of tea in front of me and took a seat at the table.

"I know, which is what gave me the idea."

"It may help your hip too. I know you still get pain in it."

"Yeah, I thought of that as well."

"I'm glad you got so much out of it."

"So, how were things here?"

She told me about another game that Missy made up. I would ask her to show me how to play tomorrow. She also shared with me about her business.

"And I am thinking about hiring another employee. I just can't believe how things have been booming."

"That's amazing." I sipped my tea. "I'm so very proud of you. You have done great things."

"Thanks, Mama."

We continued chatting and drinking our tea. It was nice, a perfect end of the evening. By the time we said good night, I was relaxed and knew it would be a good night's sleep.

Chapter Twelve

We were gearing up for Missy's birthday. It was just a week away, and she was bubbling over with excitement.

"I want everything to be perfect, Mama."

"Yes, ma'am."

We were at the party supply store picking out all the streamers, balloons, and all things you need for a five year old's birthday party. We were currently picking out stuff for the goody bags.

"Everyone at my school loves this slime. Oh, and these pencils." She picked through the pencils, selecting several different ones. "Can we add stickers? What about these?"

She was in heaven. I just nodded and let her get anything she thought would be good but stopped her once we had about six items per child. We then headed to the candy aisle for a couple of bags of candy.

With our shopping cart nearly overflowing, I pushed it to the checkout. This was going to cost a small fortune, but I had a lot of birthdays to make up for. Davy's would be in two months, and he also had big plans in the works.

"I hope we got everything, Missy." A smile spread across my face as I looked down at her.

"I think so." She looked through the cart as we waited in line. "Plates, cups, napkins. We have streamers and balloons. Tablecloths too."

"Next?" The cashier called us.

She started scanning everything, and I watched as the total climbed. Looking over at Missy's animated face made me forget to worry about the money, and even when the final tally was read, I simply scanned my card without care.

After the party store, we headed back to Glenn Lake and straight to Mary's Bakery. She would make the cake for us, and we said once we had the colors picked, we'd let her know.

Missy chatted the whole drive back.

"And everyone in my class is so excited about the party. Olive is coming and Darla too. They are my best friends. Then there is Ava and Lily, and Aiden. Oh, but Joey can't come. He has a family thing. That's what his Mama said."

I tried not to laugh from the front seat. She was so cute. I'm so glad I had this time with her. Davy was spending time with Jimmy, and Mandy was working, so it was just my youngest daughter and me to run these errands.

When we pulled up at the bakery, Missy could barely contain her excitement.

"I've never had a fancy cake before."

I took her hand, and we walked into the store, the chime over the door announcing us.

"Hiya, Missy. Hi Becca." Mary's cheerful voice greeted us.

She gave instructions to Jade and then came around the counter with her portfolio and order book.

"Let's have a seat over here."

We joined her at a table at the far side of the store, away from the busy door and counter.

"Okay, little lady, what can I make for you?"

"We brought you these." She handed Mary a plate and a napkin in the colors of her party. "This is the green I like and this pink."

"Oh, wow, these are beautiful colors." She took the plate and napkin, examining them. "I have some ideas."

She pulled out her portfolio book and flipped through a few pages. "How about this one?"

I looked at Missy, watching her while she studied the picture. She was tapping her finger on her lips.

"I like this one, but does it say 'Missy'?"

Mary and I exchanged a look and stifled laughs.

"Alright, I have a few more."

We spent the next few minutes flipping through pictures and discussing each, mostly Missy.

"This is it! This is the one."

She was pointing at a two layer wedding cake with ruffles all over it. It was gorgeous, but how grand would her actual wedding cake be if she wanted this for her fifth birthday?

"This would be perfect for you," Mary told her. "I can definitely make this one for you."

"You're too sweet, Mary," I said.

We got all the details written down, and I paid. I think I got a nice discount, but Mary didn't say. The price just seemed a bit lower than I would have thought.

"Well, I'll see you tomorrow," I said as we left.

We stopped at Alonzo's Pizza, grabbing two large pizzas, and then headed home.

"Mama, I had fun today. Thank you."

"You are so welcome, and I had fun too." I looked at her in the rearview mirror.

We pulled up at home just as Mandy and Jimmy each pulled up separately.

"Good timing." We all said almost in unison and then laughed.

They helped me bring in all the party supplies and the pizza. Missy had started telling them all about everything we picked out and her cake.

"And, Ms. Mary says she can make me my dream cake. It is going to be pink and green and ruffly."

"I want cake," Davy said.

"You have to wait. It's for my party."

"I want cake today." He pouted.

"Well, how about pizza instead?"

"Yeah, pizza!" He said, running to the table.

Later, after the pizza was eaten, we all played one of the many games that Missy made up. They were always fun, yet at times confusing.

"Mama, you can't move your guy there. You have to go that way." She instructed me to move the other way around the board.

"Okay, okay. I think I got it now."

"Wait, does that mean my little guy has to go here?" Jimmy asked as he pointed to the home space.

"Um, yes! Daddy wins."

We played again, and this time Davy won. I never won her games because, honestly, I never could figure them out. The rules on each game were always the same and consistent. She had a great imagination and could come up with fun games.

"Well, I better go," Jimmy said, standing.

He hugged each of the little kids, and then Mandy walked him out.

"That means it's time for baths."

I got Davy in first while Missy brushed her teeth, then they switched. After baths, it was story time and then lights out. Mandy came to kiss them good night, and then she got on her computer to work, and I went to the kitchen to bake.

Once again, I was thankful for Mandy's routine and that I had found a purpose in life, which kept me from thinking and feeling. That is why I used to drink, but now, just like in my group therapy, I didn't think about my stressors if I kept myself busy enough. Like the upcoming trial or my loneliness.

Saturday morning, the day of Missy's fifth birthday party, started out a bit cloudy, and I was thinking the weather forecast may end up going from thirty percent chance of rain to one hundred percent. I stared out the front window trying to wish the clouds away and the sun to come up.

"Oh no, I hope it clears before her party." Mandy joined me to stare out the window. "She will be so disappointed."

"I know. I was thinking the same." I walked down the hallway to wake up the birthday girl. "Good morning, my five year old!"

She woke up with a big smile on her face.

"Hi, Mama. It's my birthday! Yay, yay, yay. I'm five!" She jumped up and hugged me.

"Yes, you are. How does it feel?" She got a serious look on her face like she was thinking very deeply.

"It feels like... like... I have to pee."

She jumped up and ran down the hall. I laughed and then looked over at Little Davy, who was sitting up grinning.

Once they were both up, I got them breakfast. Missy talked almost non stop about who would be at her party, about the decorations, the food, and every little detail. She talked about the same topic for more than a week, and I had it memorized, but I still acted like it was the first time I heard it.

After they ate, I sent them to get dressed, brush their teeth and hair, and get shoes on. It was still a little early to leave, so Mandy and I gathered up all the party supplies and had the little kids help us get it all in the car.

"Mama, can we just go? Please? If I don't at least get there, I might die from the excitement." So dramatic. I checked the time. We'd be early but not too early.

"Okay, okay, we don't want you to die of excitement on your birthday." I tickled her.

The four of us hopped in the car, kids buckled into car seats, and then we headed to the park. Missy and Davy sang the whole way. It was a birthday song they made up.

"It's your birthday. It's my birthday. It's his birthday. It's her birthday. Everyone birthday!"

Now imagine that on repeat. It was cute for about a block. Okay, they were my kids, so it was cute for about two, but soon I wanted to jump out of the car. Instead, I tried something less dramatic.

"How about we sing something else? What about the Wheels on the Bus?"

"But that's not a very birthday song!"

And so, the annoying birthday song continued. Mandy and I rolled our eyes at each other while smiling. She was thinking the same as me, but neither of us could get them on another song.

I decided to focus on the to do list for the day. First, we would get there and decorate the pavilion. Jimmy was meeting us with the food. We were keeping it simple with hamburgers and hot dogs. He had a grill that he was able to load in his truck. Mary was going to come over later with the cake.

Thankfully, by the time we got to the park, the clouds were starting to clear a bit, and the sun was shining through them, and the most annoying song in the world stopped. It was looking like it was going to be a gorgeous day.

Jimmy and his buddy Ty were unloading his grill when we pulled up.

"Daddy! Daddy! Guess what? I'm five! I'm five!" She had unbuckled from her booster seat the second I stopped the car and ran full speed to him.

"I know, sweetie. Happy birthday."

He swung her around and then kissed her head as he set her on the ground. She ran over to Ty to tell him how old she was. He was already wrestling with Little Davy, who was giggling. The kids really liked him.

Mandy walked over with a box of decorations and said hello to Jimmy. They gave each other a sweet kiss. He then took the box from her, and they walked over to one of the picnic tables, chatting easily. When she laughed at something he said, I had a ping of jealousy run through me.

The jealousy came because of how easy their relationship seemed, not because I'd wanted Jimmy back. He wasn't the one I was in love with and probably never truly was.

She'd been unsure in the beginning for a variety of reasons. He was my ex boyfriend and the father of her siblings. However, it didn't seem like such a weird thing if you saw them together. They were perfect and a much better match than he and I ever were.

Sometimes I think the Universe played a cruel joke on all of us by making him meet me first.

At least today, I'd get to spend time with Ricky, so I really didn't have anything to be jealous about. We would have to be careful about physical contact and not flaunt our relationship since I knew Amelia would be watching us carefully.

From talking to Ricky, she was still having a difficult time with him dating, and of course, she was missing her mom. With all the changes in her life right now, I could understand it. But having lost my parents, it was a hole that was hard to fill, even with my less than loving parents.

We got to work turning the pavilion into Missy's pink and mint green dream. Balloons and streamers were everywhere. We added a birthday banner and tablecloths. As we wrapped up decorating, the bounce house, face painters, and the petting zoo arrived. Mandy and I showed them all where to set up.

Jimmy and Ty got the grill going just as the first people started to arrive. Soon the park was teeming with Missy's classmates, running, laughing, and squealing with joy. I greeted the parents. Some I knew, some I didn't. Mary arrived with the cake, and we placed it on a table near the gifts.

"Mary, it is gorgeous. Thank you! She is going to love it."

It was a pink and mint green confection and exactly what Missy had wanted. Two stacked layers of strawberry cake with fluffy frosting ruffles in alternating pink and mint green cascading down each.

She'd also included a couple dozen matching cupcakes. They looked too beautiful to eat. How did she get ruffles so delicate on each cupcake? It was purely amazing. It was wonderful of her to do those for us also since we hadn't ordered them.

"Oh, Mary, you shouldn't have! Thank you so much. These cupcakes are perfect."

"Oh, pish posh, you have more than doubled my business. Consider it my thank you to you."

"That's so sweet."

We hugged on it. I felt a lot less alone at that moment. I knew I had Mary in my corner. I'd have to remember that when the feelings of loneliness crept up on me.

Ricky, Rosa, and the kids showed up. When Missy and Olive saw that Darla had arrived, they ran over to her, squealing. They greeted each other, speaking quickly and all at once, then ran off hand in hand in hand. A friendship so innocent and straightforward. All the grown ups smiled after them.

"Hey, Becca." He came over and kissed my cheek.

Amelia gave me a dirty look. I tried to smile at her, but she turned her back on me. Ricky either didn't notice or ignored her.

"Mom, I want you to meet Mandy." He gestured to my right, where Mandy was standing. When Mandy turned to face her, Rosa gasped.

"Oh my, she does look like Maria. Wow." She stepped forward and then stopped herself. "Oh my, I'm sorry. Where are my manners? Nice to meet you, Mandy."

"Nice to meet you."

Watching grandmother and granddaughter's first meeting, I got a little choked up. They hugged then moved away from the group, speaking easily as they headed towards the drink coolers.

"Mel, why don't you take Tomas to the bounce house?" Ricky set Tomas down, and Amelia gave me one last look before taking his hand and walking him to the bounce house.

"If looks could kill," I said once they were out of earshot.

"She'll get there. She is already doing a little better at home, at least. We are talking more, and she's starting to smile and laugh with me again too." He paused, looking towards the bounce house. "She's just worried about me forgetting her mom."

He had mentioned this before, but I was glad to hear they were talking and that he felt good about things.

"I can understand that."

"Wow, everything is so..." He looked around.

"Pink and green. I mean, mint green. Missy would have my head if I said it wrong."

"Yeah." He turned and put his arms around me, smiling down at me. "God, you're gorgeous."

I blushed and thanked him, then looked around nervously, not wanting Amelia to catch us. She would definitely not like this.

More guests arrived. I greeted each, pointing them towards drinks and appetizers. Then showed them where to put gifts and directed kids towards face painters, the petting zoo, or encouraged them to join in the bounce house. I had never played host like this before. It was fun.

His sister Maria, her husband Carl, and their four kids arrived. It was so good to have family. Maria and I joined Rosa and Mandy plus Kate while the men gathered around the grill talking about baseball and discussing the still a few months away football season.

Soon, Jimmy signaled that food was ready, so we started gathering kids to eat. Parents helped fix plates for their own children and then settled the kids in seats. Missy wanted Olive on one side and Darla on the other. Everyone was happy and chatting, eating, and laughing.

I took it all in. Like my own children, I rarely had a birthday party. The few I did have were for my parents' benefit, not mine. The guest list was all the influential people my dad needed to schmooze to succeed in his career.

Once all the kiddos finished their hot dog or burger, we moved on to the cake. Missy clapped with joy at the cake, declaring it the prettiest cake in the world. She hugged Mary, thanking her over and over.

I heard some of the parents ask Mary about cakes, and a few placed orders. It looked like another win for Mary's Bakery. She caught my eye and winked. I knew she must be thinking the same.

Everyone sang happy birthday. Missy stood on one of the picnic benches so she could see everyone clapping and cheered as they sang. She then blew out the candles.

We cut the cake, and each guest got to pick either a piece of cake or a cupcake. The smiling faces of the kids and parents signaled success to me. I looked over at Mary, who was quite pleased with how her cake turned out, not just the increase in business. She nodded and smiled at me as she took another bite.

I smiled and looked back at my five-year-old birthday girl. She was laughing with her two best friends as they finished their cupcakes.

My heart warmed, watching her. I was thankful to get this moment after having missed so many, too many of them. This was wonderful, and I loved every minute of it.

I looked around the pavilion at all the faces I knew and loved. Mandy, both little kids, Ricky, Caroline, Rosa, Mary, and so many friends and neighbors.

It was then time for presents. Missy carefully unwrapped and opened each package and envelope. She made sure she knew who each was from and that they got to see her opening their gift. She thanked them, each with a hug, a smile, or a high five.

I was so proud of how she handled it. She was so thoughtful. I'm sure this was something she had learned from Mandy.

After a few hours of partying, parents started to gather their tired kids and head out of Glenn Lake Park. Missy made sure to thank everyone for coming.

As the last of the guests left, we started to clean up. Ricky stayed behind to help. We had been careful all day to not have any personal contact, and Amelia had been sure to keep a close eye on me all day.

"Thanks for helping with clean up," I said as Ricky and I were carrying gifts to the car. The kids played while Jimmy, Ty, and Mandy loaded the grill back into Jimmy's truck.

"My pleasure." He said, pulling me against him. "Speaking of my pleasure..." He leaned forward to kiss me.

"You... you... You bitch! You're trying to take my mommy's place." She burst into tears and ran towards the playground.

I hadn't seen her come up behind us. We all stood there, shocked for a moment.

"I'll go after her." Mandy took off after Amelia.

"I'm so sorry. I don't know what got into her."

"She saw you kiss me."

"I should go after her." He said, looking off into the distance.

"No, let Mandy try."

We continued to clean up while keeping one eye out for Mandy and Amelia. Even though I didn't feel like I'd done anything wrong, I had an overwhelming feeling of guilt. I didn't want to steal her mom's place and would never do that to anyone. I knew the pain of losing your mother. Even if mine wasn't the most loving like hers was, it still hurt to not have that connection, that relationship.

Finally, Mandy came back with a red faced, puffy eyed Amelia. She gave me another dirty look and walked straight to their car. I guess she was still upset, but at least she came back on her own.

"I talked to her, and she is very upset at seeing you kiss. I don't think she is ready to talk about it, but I at least got her this far."

"Thanks, Mandy. Becca, I'll call you later." He gathered up Darla and Tomas. Rosa and Mandy said a rushed goodbye and had plans to meet soon for lunch.

"Mama, why is Amelia always so upset?" Missy asked as we walked to our car. "And, you know, she said a bad word."

"Yes, she did, but you know they lost their mom last year."

It was on the tip of my tongue to ask if they would be upset to lose me, but I suspect they would be okay with Mandy, as they were months ago when I left them.

We got Davy and Missy strapped in their booster seats and headed home. Davy was knocked out before we got more than a block from the park. Missy chatted away about this friend or that gift or how the rabbits from the petting zoo were so soft.

I tried to focus on what Missy was saying, but my mind was elsewhere. I really hoped things would be okay with Ricky and Amelia. I hated being the source of drama for them. Though, again, I didn't feel like I'd done anything wrong.

Didn't I have the right to date him? Shouldn't he get to choose his friends? I hoped he was able to help her find peace in this. I hated to see her upset.

We got home, and I carried Davy into bed before bringing all the gifts and extra party supplies into the house. Missy was helpful.

"Did you have a nice day?" I asked her as we settled on the couch together.

"It was the bestest day. Thank you so much for everything." She leaned forward and hugged me.

"Aw, you are so very welcome. I am glad that you had a nice day."

We sat together talking about her favorite gift and her best memory from the day. It was a moment to share together and helped take my mind off of Ricky and whatever he was dealing with on his side of town.

Chapter Thirteen

The night after the party, I had trouble sleeping. I kept thinking about Amelia and the look in her eyes when she caught us kissing. Her words echoed in my head. You bitch. You're trying to take my mommy's place.

It broke my heart because the last thing I wanted was to replace their mother. From everything Ricky had told me, Sonya sounded like a wonderful woman and an even better mom. The kind of mother I wished I had been. The kind of mother I was trying to become. I would never try to erase her memory or take her place in those children's hearts.

But I wanted to be happy too. I wanted my second chance at love with the man I had never stopped loving. Was that so wrong? It was complicated even for me to sort through, so how could I expect an eight year old to understand it? She was just a little girl who missed her Mama. I couldn't blame her for that.

However, the lack of sleep meant the morning would come early, making for a long day, but I at least managed to sleep a few hours.

I didn't have a text from Ricky in the morning either. Maybe he was sleeping in. It was Sunday, and the restaurant didn't open for several hours. I wasn't worried yet.

Okay, perhaps a little worried, but I would keep my mind busy and not focus on it. He would text when he could. I was almost positive about it.

I got to the bakery a little early, so I had to wait for Mary to unlock the shop. She lived above it in an apartment, so she had a short commute to work. Though it didn't look like she was up yet or at least not ready to open the shop.

As I waited for her, I had time to think. My mind drifted back to Amelia. I hoped she was okay. I hoped Ricky had been able to comfort her last night. It couldn't be easy for her to see her dad with someone else, especially after such a tragic loss.

I saw the lights come on in the store and Mary at the door, so I grabbed my things. I was halfway to the door loaded down with my baked goods when I heard my text chime. I jumped and nearly dropped everything. Then my heart started pounding, and I hoped it was Ricky. I couldn't check, though, as I was loaded down with goodies. So it would have to wait.

"Good morning, Becca. Let me get some of these from you. Do you have more in the car?" Mary said from the door.

"Thanks. I do."

We got the first load into the shop and went back for the others. I got right to work slicing and stocking the display case, and then customers arrived in droves before we barely had the sign flipped to open. The line had started forming at quarter to the hour.

It was hours before I even remembered that I had received a text and had time to check my phone. Everything I brought had sold, and I was in the kitchen making more. It was only then during that semi alone time that my mind remembered the text.

Unfortunately, I was busy baking, and I still couldn't check. But if it was Ricky, I hoped he wasn't worried that I hadn't replied yet. I would as soon as I could.

Once I got everything baking in the oven and the dishes done, I finally checked the text. It was from Ricky, wishing me a good morning. I replied.

He replied later that evening. The uncertainty that I would hear from him again melted away as we texted off and on the rest of the night. Nothing earth shattering, just goofy back and forth small talk.

The next day was my counseling appointment. I had moved them to Mondays since Mary was closed on Mondays. It made things easier, so I didn't have to take off and could work more days.

"Okay, Becca, how have things been this week?"

"Fine. Things have been fine."

"Last time you were telling me that your ex boyfriend had come back into your life and he had found out about Mandy. How is all that going?"

"Well, we are kinda dating again. He and Mandy have met and are starting to get to know each other. His mom has also met Mandy too. It all seems to be going well. Except his eight year old daughter isn't thrilled, but he is talking to her about it."

"Okay, interesting. Why don't you tell me about things when you were dating before? What do you think happened?"

I thought back for a moment before telling her about my parents. They were the biggest problem, and I knew that they were a huge obstacle for Ricky and me to be together. Not to mention his going away to college, but I think I would have worked harder to be with him had they not been so adamant about us not being together.

"It all started when I was fourteen and had been dating Ricky for a few months or so..."

They had called me to the living room. My mother was perched on the edge of the sofa, and my father was in his chair like a king sitting on his throne. In a way, he was, and he ruled with an iron fist.

"Rebecca, we want to talk to you about that boy." My father was the only one that called me Rebecca versus my nickname of Becca.

"Ricky?"

"Yes, him." He sat forward. "We forbid you from seeing him."

"What? Why?" I could feel my heart being crushed.

"We just don't approve of him or his family. He is not like us." With his statement, he sat back again.

"Like us? Like us, how? What do you mean?"

"He is one of those illegals. The ones from Mexico." My mother whispered as if people could hear us.

We were sitting in our own house, and there was nobody else around. So really, it was one of those judgmental and embarrassed whispers. It was disgusting for her to even think that.

"He isn't illegal. He and most of his family were born here and are US citizens. His great grandmother Carmen married a US citizen who just happened to be a Mexican, and then she became a citizen herself shortly after moving here to be with him. They are just as legal as you and me."

At my words, my mother gasped and fell back. Dramatics were her specialty. My father sat straight up.

"Now you listen, and you listen good. That boy is bad news, and you will NOT see him again. Do you understand me?"

"He is a wonderful, caring person who saved me, and I will not stop seeing him. I love him, and he loves me. He plans to marry me after he finishes college." I was on the verge of tears.

My mother had fainted, but it was all fake. She always did this.

However, my father jumped to his feet and pulled his belt off in one swift motion. He started hitting me. Face, arms, legs. To him, it didn't matter as long as he was hitting me. Discipline, he called it discipline.

"Now you listen to me." He continued hitting me as he spoke. "I will not repeat myself. You will not see that boy again. Do you understand me?"

I had to agree, or he would have just kept hitting me until I did agree with him. I had no intention of ending things with Ricky. I would just have to sneak around to see him.

Once the discipline stopped, I ran to the semi safety of my room, and I cried myself to sleep. I woke the next day with bruises, a broken heart, and hate for my father. I didn't understand why they had a child if they didn't love me. It was like I was a possession to him, really to both of them, or perhaps something they were obligated to have.

You have a house, jobs, cars, go to church, and you have a child. At least that seemed the way, according to Wade and Beth Morgan.

"How did this all lead to breaking up with Ricky? And why did you hide your pregnancy from him?"

"Gosh, those are tough questions." I just started talking about the first thing that came to mind.

I did continue to see Ricky, and a few months later, in March, I found out I was pregnant. I took the test at Stephanie's house. She held my hand while we waited to see if there would be one line or two. There were two. She cried with me.

"Steph, what am I going to do? My parents are going to kill me, especially since it's Ricky's. And I can't tell him. He will stay here and not go to college. He will be the first in his family to go, and he has that scholarship. I can't let him throw all that away for me." I was sobbing scared, bitter tears.

She didn't have an answer, and I didn't expect her to. I was only fourteen and would be a fifteen year old mother. What had I done? Many would say I made the grown up decision to have sex, which I did, so I needed to deal with grown up consequences, which I also knew I did. It still didn't mean I knew what to do, just that I knew this was something I had done, and I couldn't hide it forever. There would be a baby in seven months, and there was no hiding that fact.

I bought some multivitamins and started taking those immediately because I knew I needed the extra for myself and the baby. However, it took me more than a month to tell my parents. I needed to because they would find out sooner or later, and I probably needed to see a doctor for the baby.

I guessed I was nearly four months pregnant when I was finally ready to tell my parents. I told them I needed to talk to them. My mother rolled her eyes, and my father barely gave me the time of day, but I was insistent, so they finally sat in the living room. This is where we always had our serious talks.

"Mom, dad. This isn't easy for me to tell you, but..." My heart was beating so fast. They were going to beat me black and blue. I just hoped it didn't hurt the baby. I didn't know much about him or her, but I knew I loved them. "I am pregnant."

"What?" My father jumped straight to his feet with his hand on his belt. "Who is the father? It better not be that boy."

"Hmm, no, no, I was... I was raped. I don't know the boy at all. It was a party, and I didn't know everyone there." I really hoped they bought this. I thought it was better than saying it was Ricky's. Maybe they would forgive me.

"You little slut. You probably asked for it. The way you dress and act, you probably let him." How could a father say those things about his daughter? My mother, of course, was playing up the dramatics.

She was fanning herself and repeating, "Oh my goodness. Oh, my goodness."

"I didn't let him. He raped me."

"Well, I will not have a baby in this house. You will have to get an abortion or get out of my house. Your choice."

"I am not going to have an abortion. I am going to have this baby. It is a baby... I can't... that is murder... Isn't it?"

I started crying. If I had been raped, I might have considered it, but it was Ricky's. I loved him, and I already loved this baby. I had every intention of keeping it, even though I didn't know what else I was going to do. That was the one thing I was sure of.

"Then you are no longer welcome here. You are allowed to pack one bag, but most everything belongs to us." He was so cold. How could a father turn his back on his only daughter? My mother was utterly useless as she had faked a fainting spell.

I cried as I packed. My mother was tasked with supervising, so I didn't take anything they deemed to be theirs, and she took her job very seriously. She took things away from me as I tried to pack. She only allowed basic clothing and some toiletries.

She also kept saying things like, "How am I going to show my face around town? I can't believe I raised such a slutty daughter. What a disappointment?" It all just made me cry a little harder.

Stephanie said her parents would let me stay with them. I wasn't sure how long I could stay or what I would do if I didn't get to stay.

Once I finished packing, my father took my house key away from me, then turned his back on me and walked away without a word. My mother had fainted on the couch again, so she was useless.

Gee, thanks, folks, for fourteen years of hell. Thanks for the beautiful send off.

I walked the couple of blocks to Stephanie's house, and that was it. My life had changed. Once I got there, I did call Ricky to let him know so that he didn't call my house or come over to sneak me out that night. I didn't tell him why, just that I had had a fight with my parents, and they kicked me out. My plan was to keep the pregnancy a secret for as long as I could. I knew my parents wouldn't gossip about it. As long as I could keep it a secret, then nobody would know.

"So, how did you end things with Ricky? Why?"

"I just told him that I couldn't see him anymore. I told him my parents wouldn't let me move back home until I ended things with him. Of course, it wasn't true, but I had to end things somehow, and that was the only way I could. He would have stayed, and I would have felt so guilty had I stood in his way."

I sighed and twisted the hem of my shirt as I thought about what to say. "He did get his degree. He has been successful. I'm happy that he did. His family was so proud of him for finishing college. I remember hearing about it through the small town grapevine. They had written a whole article about him in the hometown paper. That's a big deal in a small place like Glenn Lake. By then, Mandy was nearly five years old, and I was just moving back. My father had just died."

I didn't continue my thoughts. Instead, I looked at her, tears in my eyes.

She didn't ask any additional questions. She just had a few closing comments, and then we wrapped up. I scheduled my next session for two weeks from today.

I had a long drive home, so I could think on the way. I felt spent. All the emotions of that year had bubbled up. It was a lot for one day, but that was the point of counseling, I supposed.

When I got back into town, I wanted to see Ricky. He was better than searching for comfort in a bottle. So I messaged him to see if he was working. He didn't answer, so I drove over to the restaurant. His car was there, so I parked and headed inside. Rosa greeted me with a hug and kiss on each cheek.

"Is Ricky busy?"

"He might be, but go on back. He's probably washing dishes or something in the kitchen."

I walked back. Loretta and Martin waved as I passed through the dining room. I got to the kitchen, and Abuelita Carmen was making tortillas. She smiled and winked at me. I smiled in return, and then I saw Ricky. He was washing dishes, his favorite thing to do at the restaurant.

My breath caught, and my pulse quickened. That man was hot. I took in the sight of him for just a second, never tiring of watching him. It was something I used to do years ago, just stand and watch him work.

"Becca, hi. What are you doing here?" He dried his hands as he walked towards me, then wrapped me in his arms. Tears sprung to my eyes.

"This. I needed this." My voice was shaky.

"Rough day?"

"You could say that."

"Let's step out to chat." He released me so we could walk out the back door.

Once outside, he put his arms around me again and kissed the top of my head. I let out the tears that had been threatening to fall. He just held me, letting me cry it out. He didn't try to make me talk about it, just held me through it. When I had cried myself down to just a few sniffles, he dropped his arms to my hands.

"Better?"

"Yes. Thank you. I just had an extremely uncomfortable, real counseling session. I know that's the point, but it was just reliving some things I would as soon forget. The very things I had been drinking to forget. You know?"

"I get it, babe. I'm here for you now, and just think of how much stronger you are going to be once you get through all this."

That made me smile. Then he leaned over and kissed me. I melted. God, I loved this man.

He walked me back through to the front door of the restaurant and then out to my car. He told me he would text me later, kissed me once more, and then we said goodbye.

I headed for home but first swung through Emilio's deli to grab a sandwich for lunch. I messaged Mandy to see if she was on a lunch break. She replied that she would be soon and would love a sandwich. Emilio's had the best potato salad, so I ordered a small to go with our sandwiches.

I pulled up just as Mandy was getting out of her car.

"Hey, Mama. Thanks for grabbing lunch. I love Emilio's!"

"No problem. I got us some potato salad too."

"You read my mind."

We headed in and set the table for lunch. Mandy grabbed us some iced tea while I laid out the sandwiches and potato salad.

"So, how was counseling?"

"Hmm, a little rough today, but it will be worth it, I think. I hope."

"Yeah, I hope so. I want that for you."

She was the sweetest, most loving daughter. I couldn't believe how quickly she had forgiven me for everything. I didn't deserve her. I honestly didn't.

"I don't deserve you. You are an incredible person."

"Aw, Mama." She smiled and looked a little embarrassed.

We continued to chat as we finished our lunch. She had to get back to work, so I told her I would clean up lunch. I then started working on baking for work tomorrow.

Chapter Fourteen

The next few weeks were quiet and uneventful, which was good. A much needed break for my emotions and a chance to give my brain a rest. My next counseling session had gone better after revealing so much to Lisa the previous weeks. She was able to break open some of my deeper feelings and motivations for my behaviors. I felt more relieved than emotionally spent and sad after this session, which was a nice change.

There was no drama with Ricky and Amelia. He said she was trying to be more open to the idea, and they were talking each night about her feelings, her life, and he was also getting her back into counseling. I helped get a recommendation from my therapist. She gave me the name of an excellent child psychologist who specialized in childhood trauma, so I passed that on to Ricky.

Things weren't perfect, but they were going in the right direction, so I shouldn't have been surprised by the sudden turn of events as Butch's trial started to get closer and was getting a lot of media time. People, especially those close to the family, expected me to be charged as an accessory.

I was devastated, to say the least. I hadn't even wanted to be in that car with him. Of course, I wouldn't have been if he hadn't hit me and dragged me into it.

Not all my injuries were from the car wreck, and according to the doctors, being partially unconscious might have saved my life. My body wasn't tense like you might be right before an accident, so it wasn't trying to fight the impact or something like that. Crazy.

I had been working with the district attorney and the police to get him the maximum sentence possible, not just for killing the family, but we were adding charges for the domestic abuse I suffered. People didn't know that minor detail. They just knew that I was in the car and also drunk and wanted justice for that family.

I promise I did too. I might have made too many bad choices in my life, but I never drank and drove. I was planning to take a cab from the bar that night and had already called for one.

I was starting to get phone calls and people driving by the house shouting all kinds of things. Murderer was their favorite. It was at all hours of the night. I was thankful the children were good sleepers.

Others were protesting in front of Mary's. She would chase them off with a broom. She was like a pit bull. Protective, loyal, and feisty. You don't mess with Ms. Mary, and those crowds found out quickly. They would just move a little farther down the street but where they could still see the shop and me.

The Sheriff posted a deputy outside to keep the crowds under control and had them follow me home. I hated that I was bringing so much negative attention to Glenn Lake.

Those that knew me understood the situation and were on my side. I was so fortunate that many in town were fighting them on my behalf. That is one thing I loved about Glenn Lake. We took care of our own here.

"Mary, I'm so sorry this is coming here to the shop. At least the trial is soon, and then hopefully, it will all be over."

"Oh, sweetie pie, it's fine. I get it. I raised a gay son in this small town as a single mom. Come on, I have seen trouble before." She laughed it off with a flip of her hand.

I didn't feel that blasé about it. This was sure to be a setback with my plan of progressing my life forward. I felt so anxious, and after finally being able to sleep, I struggled with it again.

Instead of sleeping, I would sit near the window, just peeking out the side of the blinds. Hoping nobody would see me. Hoping nobody would shoot or throw anything through the windows.

"I'm thinking of having Jimmy take the kids until this blows over. I hate to. They are just starting to trust me, especially Davy, but I know being a mom means protecting them. What do you think?"

"Yes, I agree. It sucks to not have them as y'all are trying to rebuild relationships, but it is safer for them." She hugged me. "You can get through this. You have a big cheering section. As in most of Glenn Lake."

Thankfully, we still had lines of paying customers at the shop, so it wasn't impacting Mary's bottom line. I was relieved because I didn't want to bring my personal problems to work.

Every single local that came in would tell me they had my back and were on my side. However, when Ms. Graham came into the shop, she had an impressive plan.

"Becca, I'm so glad you're here. I have been trying to catch up to you and keep missing you, even at home."

"Oh hi, Caroline. What's going on?"

"Well, I thought you should hold a press conference. Tell your side of the story. Maybe with the district attorney's office, or we could hire a lawyer."

"You're a genius. That could be a good idea. All people really know right now is that I was drinking and in the car. They don't know that I was nearly beat into a coma even before getting in that car and then forced into the car."

"And I would be happy to help. I used to do press releases and have worked with the media before." She said.

"Great. I'll stop by after work, and we can talk about it more."

"I'll have tea ready." She bought some cookies and a few slices of my quick bread before leaving.

I was so appreciative of her offer to help me. I wanted my life back. I couldn't go anywhere without being harassed, not out in public, not at home, and not even online. People sent me nasty messages or posted to news stories.

There was even a petition online seeking to have charges brought against me and wanted them to pursue the death penalty. Butch wasn't even being charged with the death penalty.

It looked like the most he could be sentenced with would be up to twenty years because of how he was charged. So why were people hoping I would be arrested and sentenced more than the actual driver?

I was trying so hard to put my life back together and was anxious to get this bump in the road behind me. For the most part, I had. I had a job, my kids, and I hadn't had a drink since the night of the accident. I was reunited with Ricky, and the biggest secret of my life had been exposed. Finally, it felt like I was in the right place in life.

I knew I still had work to do on myself, and I would through my counseling and various group meetings, but I felt more like the self I knew I should have, could have been had my life not gone off the rails so badly. I was finally finding myself.

Caroline and I worked out a plan. Then, while still at her house, I called the DA's office to tell him our proposal.

"So, I thought if I told my side of things, it might get these protests and petitions to stop."

"What did you have in mind?"

"A press conference. Call the various news stations and tell my version of things."

"And you think this will stop the angry mob?"

"I sure hope so."

"I'll get it set up and let you know when."

We disconnected, and I turned to look at Caroline.

"Thank you so much for your help. You don't know what this means to have so many people on my side. I have never felt like I had that."

"Oh, sweetie, you have always had people on your side. You just didn't see it."

"I know... I mean, I know now." I wiped a lone tear that fell from my eye. "You helped Mandy so much, and she wouldn't be who she is today without you. That is the best thing you could have done for me."

We chatted a bit longer before I headed back to my house. There were people nearby, but so was Deputy Smith. I waved to him, and he nodded. We had gone to school together. The people started shouting at me immediately. I just kept my head down and walked into my house.

Once inside, I put my back to the door and slid to the floor. God, this was exhausting. I wanted a drink so badly right now. I know that wasn't the answer, but the feeling to escape was so overwhelming. I didn't want to think or feel. I wanted to drink enough to sleep a deep, dreamless sleep.

I sat there, head in my hands, crying my heart out, letting all my old wounds open and the pain seep out as tears. This plan had to work. I needed these people off my lawn, out of my town, and out of my life. All of their shouting was too much.

It was just too much, but I pulled myself up and dried my eyes. I could do this. I was stronger than I used to be, and I knew it.

"You got this, Becca. You are not that same little girl anymore." Yes, I thought. New me, new life. No looking back, only forward.

It was a quarter to five, so I headed to the kitchen to start prepping for dinner. Mandy would be home with the little kids soon.

I hadn't cooked much before the accident, but now I had learned that I actually enjoyed it. It was one more way I was healing.

I was nearly done cooking when the crowd start up again. Mandy and the kids must be home. Thankfully, Deputy Smith was still there. His voice amplified by the bullhorn.

I went to the door to open it for them. The little kids looked so confused. I knew then that I had to let them go to Jimmy's. So tonight, I would make that happen.

"Mama!" They both ran to me and gave me huge hugs.

"I missed you, babies, today. How was school?"

Missy launched into a full recap of the day. This was one of my favorite parts of the day, hearing about their day.

"And Olive had her hair up in pigtails, and Darla was sad because she wanted pigtails in her hair. Sooo Ms. Lyndsey put it up for her. I didn't care. I liked the braid that you did for my hair today." She touched her hair as she spoke.

It was a simple braid, nothing fancy, but I'm glad she liked it.

"I played with Ryan. He my bestest friend. He funny, Mama." Little Davy said, then put his arms up so I would pick him up.

God, this was going to be so hard to let them go, even if I knew it would be temporary. We were making such progress in rebuilding, or should I say building, our relationships and bond.

"And, Mama, why do those people keep yelling at us? Why are they here?"

I knew the question was coming, but I didn't know how to explain it. I looked at Mandy. She mouthed for me to be honest.

"Do you remember the car accident I was in?" I asked.

They both nodded.

"Well, these people are mad about it. They think I should get in trouble for being in that car because some people got hurt."

They seemed to take that as a good enough explanation because they both smiled and ran off to play in their room.

"I wasn't sure that was going to be enough of an explanation, but it seemed to be," I said to Mandy.

"Yes, they are pretty face value on things."

"So, I'm thinking about calling Jimmy and having them stay with him until it's over."

"Really? Wow." She thought for a moment. "I hate to say it, but it probably is a good idea. But how long do you think this will last?" She gestured towards the front window.

"I'm not sure yet. Maybe until after the trial, and even then, it might not let up until they feel like there is justice for that family, which I do understand. I just don't think I should have to be the one to pay the price. That should be Butch."

"I still can't believe he could only get twenty years. That's crazy in my mind."

"That's why they are hoping that adding the domestic abuse, and possibly kidnapping, could add at least a few years or at least ensure he gets the max sentencing."

All the legal terms made my head spin. If this, then that, but only if the other thing. A maze of combinations I couldn't track.

"Do you want me to call Jimmy for you?"

"Actually, yes, that would be great. If he can pick them up after dinner, so at least we can have dinner together."

I was not going to cry. I was not going to cry. Well, at least not until they were gone, and I was alone in bed.

She went to the other room to call Jimmy while I went into the kitchen to get dinner finished and on the table. As I was doing that, I could then hear her go to the kids' room to pack their things.

They were asking her a bunch of questions. At least they sounded excited about the adventure. They didn't stay with Jimmy often, even though they both had a room there. With our arrangement, they did see him almost daily. This was going to be weird, but it was in their best interest.

We ate dinner. The kids chatted about staying with daddy. I held it together and tried to hide that I was anxious and saddened by them leaving. If they noticed, they didn't let on.

As we finished eating, Jimmy showed up. We knew immediately because the crowd noise picked up. He hadn't been over yet since this had started.

"Wow, I didn't realize how bad this was. That is crazy. Glad that Deputy Smith is out there."

"Yeah, it's bad. Mary chased them away from the store today. Broom in hand." I said with a chuckle.

"That must have been a sight to see."

"Oh, it was." Then I turned to the kids. "Are y'all finished with dinner?"

"Yes, I am." Missy hopped up and cleared her plate to the kitchen sink. She was so good.

"Me too." Little Davy followed her.

Then they came over and gave me a hug. I kissed their heads and told them I would visit soon. They hugged Mandy, and Jimmy had their bags. I didn't try to walk them out.

Thankfully, Jimmy had thought to give the deputy a heads up on his way in, so he was ready to help shield the kids as much as he could. It looked like he had moved the crowd back and warned them that children were coming out, saying he would arrest any of them that yelled while the kids were present.

I also saw that a few more deputies had shown up. Were they backup? What a nightmare. Was it over yet?

I watched from the window while Jimmy got the kids into his truck without incident. I sighed with relief when they took off. Mandy put her arms around me. At least I had her by my side.

"So, now what?"

"Now, we wait for the DA to get back to me and tell me the next steps so I can tell my side of the story."

And wait, we did. It was several days before he called me back. During that time, the crowds got a little bigger, a little bolder. I was considering going into hiding myself.

Never having much alone time from the little kids before, Mandy and I took advantage of the time to bond and strengthen our relationship. The rare nights they did stay at Jimmy's, she would stay over there too. I didn't mind, really, but I loved the idea of us having this mother daughter time. It felt more like friends at her age, but maybe we would have evolved to this point anyway.

The first night alone, we gave each other pedicures and laughed over a romantic comedy.

"Just what the doctor ordered!" I sighed.

"Agreed, and I love this red. Where did you find it?" She said, admiring her toes.

"At Kay's Beauty Salon and Supplies." I smiled down at my toes too. "I'm glad we did this."

"Me too, Mama. We should do this more."

The next night we played with our hair. We laughed at the crazy hairdos we came up with for each other, and we talked about books, movies, and random other things.

We did something fun each night. It was wonderful to get to know my eldest daughter better and have a blast doing it. We learned so much more about each other.

I missed having the little kids home, but these days with Mandy were so very much needed. I was hoping this was just one more step to having a better mother daughter relationship, the kind we both wanted.

It was also the perfect distraction from the people outside the house and the media circus that was building around this trial. It gave me something else to think about and not worry about for just a few minutes.

Sleeping was still a little hard to come by. Knowing the protesters were still out there had me tossing, turning, and scared out of my mind. What if they got bold enough to do something more than just yell and march around?

I was thankful to the Sheriff and Deputies for keeping watch over us, though. I had been baking them extra goodies as thank yous, but I knew it wouldn't be enough for what they were doing.

Finally, the DA called me. I couldn't have been more relieved to hear what he had to say.

"Thank you for calling me. Unfortunately, it has gotten crazier."

"Well, good news. The Judge has approved you to speak. He was worried about the impact on the trial, but I have given your side of things to him, and he agrees that the trial is not about you and should hopefully get at least some of the people off the picket lines."

"Okay, great. So now what?"

"Now you have an appointment on Tuesday with me. We will hold a press conference in front of the courthouse downtown, and we will give a statement about your side. How you are also a victim, kidnapped, and forced into the car, et cetera. Sound good?"

"Yes, I just hope that this makes a difference. I wish this part would have come out sooner."

"I'm sorry. It should have. We are going to fix it now. I didn't know this would happen." I heard papers shuffling on his end of the call. "I'm officially going to press charges on your behalf for the domestic abuse. As you know, it wasn't in there as an official charge before. The judge will read him the new charges later today. That is why it took me a little longer to call you. We wanted to make sure that we could get the new charges approved."

"I'm so glad to hear that. Well, not glad, but relieved. I am so ready for this to be over."

We talked through a few more details before disconnecting. I had just a few more days before I could tell my story. I had to hope it would make these crowds go away.

They were starting to get bold and violent. Today several of them threw trash at me. They were immediately arrested and charged.

After the incident, a deputy was assigned to me. I hated that there were so many people put out to protect me. I had never given much to this town until recently, and what I was giving wasn't enough to warrant this special treatment.

I appreciated it, though. Small town living was the best.

Ricky had been distant the last few days or so. I wasn't sure if it was by choice or had just been busy with his kids and work.

While I could have used the extra support and one of his hugs, his absence also gave me time to process everything that was going on and think. But I missed him. He had become my safe place again.

Finally, the night before my press conference, Ricky called. My stomach fluttered when I saw his name displayed on my phone.

"I can't believe how crazy things are around town. The restaurant has been swamped." He exhaled. "We have seen all the signs and protestors. How are you holding up?"

"I'm doing okay. I miss my kids... And I miss you."

"I miss you too. Are you nervous about tomorrow?"

"A little, but I just hope it will help clear things up. I know there will still be some people who don't believe it, but the DA has Dr. Stephens speaking tomorrow. She was the doctor who initially treated me and hopes her assessment of my injuries will help change peoples' minds." I smiled to myself. "There are so many people on my side. I just want the truth to come out and my life to get back to normal."

"Do you need me to come out there with you? For extra support."

"Thanks, I think I can do it. Mandy, Ms. Graham, and Mary are going with me. Dr. Stephens will be there, and Jimmy is going to meet us there from work. I think others might drive up from Glenn Lake, but... I mean, it's up to you."

"I will see if I can get away." He said.

That gave me a little hope in us. It also gave me faith that this would turn out okay as well. I knew I had a lot of support on my side. I had new inner strength in myself, or at least I hoped I did, and that it was enough to get me through this bump in the road. I had to take this stand for myself and prayed it paid off. I wanted my children at home. I wanted my town back to normal and the people that I loved to be safe.

The next day, we were up early to head to Houston for the press conference. Unfortunately, the early hour hadn't stopped the crowds from forming. They yelled and tried to push towards us, but luckily, Sheriff Riley arrived with several deputies.

We had anticipated there would be issues, so we let them know what time we were leaving. He gave me a thumbs up as we drove past. I flashed him a thumbs up in return.

We took Caroline's car, and the three of us headed over to pick up Mary before officially making our way north. The vibe in the car was upbeat and positive. I was nervous. The reality was setting in that I would have to speak in front of a large group of people and that the live feed would be streamed into homes and onto cell phones, snapped and tweeted, retweeted, and could go viral. It made my head spin at the thought.

My phone chimed that I had a text. It was Ricky wishing me good luck. Then a few minutes later, it rang again. It was Stephanie also wishing me well. I could feel the love from my many supporters.

Okay, okay, I could do this. I just had to believe in myself like others did, I thought to myself.

We got to the DA's office. The receptionist had us take a seat for a moment while she called back to his office. A few minutes later, he came out to greet us with a handshake.

"Okay, Becca, as I told you yesterday on the phone, Butch did not take the news of the charges well, and then this morning, Butch was attacked in the showers by several other inmates and beaten." I gasped at the news. The DA nodded before continuing. "He's been taken to the hospital, alive. This is not a turn we were expecting. Apparently, the guy who initially jumped him lost his sister to domestic abuse, and he took his revenge on Butch. The others piled on."

I was in shock. I hadn't wanted Butch harmed in all this. I just wanted my name cleared, my family, and my new life back to normal.

"Wow, okay, wow. Does that change our plan and statement today?" I assumed it would.

"Not really, but maybe just to say we hope that he recovers so that he can face the charges against him and bring justice for the Jones family."

"Sounds good." The news had me a little shaken, and I hoped it didn't distract me from the mission.

Dr. Stephens arrived shortly after we did. She reviewed her notes with the DA and was debriefed on Butch before we headed to the courthouse. Then, we loaded into a city van to drive over for the press conference as one group.

Everyone chatted, making small talk, and trying to keep things in the van light, but you could feel the tension and nerves, at least amongst my group. I tried to be engaged in the conversation, but I was rehearsing what I would say.

My biggest worry was that I'd freeze up or make things worse. I had never been good at public speaking.

When we pulled up to the courthouse, my nerves were kicking big time, and the massive crowds with signs mostly protesting me had my heart beating in my ears.

There were more people here than what we'd seen in Glenn Lake. Though as I scanned the crowd, I saw some familiar faces and a few signs supporting me. That put a smile on my face, but for the most part, it was a blur of faces, and I didn't see the one I wanted to see the most.

As we exited the van, a couple of officers escorted us to the podium. We stood on the steps of the courthouse in a row behind it. Ready or not, here we go.

First, the police chief made a statement, then the DA, then Dr. Stephens, and last me. The crowd was in a roar when we arrived. Booing and screaming for the death penalty. But by the time it was my turn, it was only a soft murmur.

I stepped forward slowly, looking over at my daughter and friends, Mary and Caroline. They smiled, giving me the courage to continue. I took a deep breath and turned towards the crowd.

"I appreciate all of you here in the audience today, those that support me and even those that don't, because you are at least here to hear my side. I admit I had been drinking that night." I paused and looked around to judge reactions. "However, as you've heard, I was forced into the car against my will. I was only partially conscious at the time of the accident. When I woke up from my coma, I was very sorry to hear about the Jones family. My heart goes out to little Benji, as he will never know his parents or siblings." The crowd reacted with some sneers, but still less than initially. "Please know if I could go back and make different choices, I would. I hope that the public, the Jones family, and the city of Houston will accept my apologies. Thank you all."

This time, the crowd cheered for me. I was stunned and nearly lost my balance stepping back with the others. There were a few boos mixed in, but they were quickly drowned out.

Our little party turned and got back in the van. We were quiet for two blocks before Caroline broke the silence.

"That was excellent, dear, just excellent."

"It was. You did great, Mama." Mandy said, squeezing my hand.

"I agree. I'm so glad I closed the shop to witness this." Mary added.

"Thank you all. I really appreciate the support." I smiled at my friends and daughter.

We got back to the DA office. I thanked him and asked him to update me when he hears more about Butch's condition. I thanked Dr. Stephens for her part as well. Then we all parted ways.

When Mary, Mandy, Caroline, and I got back in the car, I turned my phone on, and it started blowing up with texts and voicemails. Steph, Ricky, Jimmy, and a few others in Glenn Lake all told me how great I had done.

I couldn't stop smiling as I read through the texts. For the first time in my life, I had stood up for myself, and it felt so amazing. I wanted to shout. I was thirty two years old, and this was truly one of the few times I remember anyone telling me they were proud of me, and I actually felt proud of myself.

When we got back to Glenn Lake, we found there were almost no angry crowds. It appeared the press conference had worked. We got Mary dropped off, and then we headed home.

Pulling up, the deputies were gone, as were the masses. It was just our quiet street again.

"Thank you so much, Caroline."

"You are so welcome, my dear." She hugged me.

She went home as Mandy and I crossed to ours.

"I think I'm going to head into town," I said as we reached the steps of our house.

"Going to see dad?"

"Maybe," I said coyly.

"Have fun, Mama."

Chapter Fifteen

After leaving the restaurant, I stopped by the store to grab supplies for work. Mary had told the Donovans to charge her shop for anything I bought for the bakery. It allowed me to buy in bulk, and I never worried about running out of supplies. It was a great system.

Mr. Donovan loaded everything in my car. "I saw your speech on TV."

"Oh, yeah? I was so nervous."

"You were great. We're all proud of you."

"Thanks, and it looks like things have settled down around town a bit."

"Yes, the most exciting thing that has happened in town for a while and didn't get too crazy."

"Agreed. Thankfully, most were fairly calm. There were a few shouting things when my kids were around and then a couple of trash throwers."

"Some people don't have basic manners."

"So true." I nodded. "Well, thank you for helping me with the groceries. Take care."

"Bye, Becca."

I headed home to get to work on my baking. Mary had said I could use the bakery kitchen, and yes, it would have been easier in many ways, but I had a system and felt most comfortable working at home. Though I did borrow several of her pans so I didn't have to buy more yet.

I had about six of my own. I borrowed another six of hers. My oven fits six at a time, so it worked out perfectly. My system started with six and worked through them until I had at least six of each type and sometimes extra banana as it was the favorite. It was hours of extra work, but it was worth it, and Mary compensated me well for my time.

When I pulled up at home, I smiled when I saw there were no longer people camped out in front of our house. I messaged Jimmy so we could get the kids home. We settled on him bringing them back the next day after school. That would work. I missed them like crazy, and it had only been a week.

I got to work on banana bread first. A few hours later, I had dozens of cooling baked goods around the kitchen and was trying to decide what to eat.

Mandy was going to eat with Jimmy and the kids, so it was just me for dinner. I landed on a peanut butter and jelly sandwich with some sliced apples. I had one leftover from the apple cinnamon bread I made. It was a new recipe I was bringing into the shop for the first time tomorrow. Fingers crossed.

I took my dinner into the living room and flipped on the TV. The Food Network was always a good choice. I watched the worst cooks learn to be better cooks by some great mentors. Halfway through, I found myself yelling at the TV.

"Why would you mix those ingredients together? Yuck!" I wasn't exactly the best cook and certainly not classically trained, but I knew some basics. Maybe a little more than the basics since I watched so many cooking shows and loved to bake.

Baking had become my saving grace and gave me something good to focus on. I never felt that I had that before. Maybe I should have felt that when I had Mandy. I guess I did at first, but life kept kicking me.

As Mandy got older, she became independent, and it seemed like she didn't need me. She raised Missy and Davy because I was so into my own life and not worrying about my three children I brought into the world. They at least had each other.

I just felt like I had no point, no purpose, no direction. I was a lost little kid who had grown up but never matured. I was always waiting for something.

Working for Mary had changed that. Finally, I had a reason to get up each morning, a place to go, and something to fill my day. I wasn't just waiting on the kids to get out of school or Mandy to get home from work. I was part of the human race, not just a spectator with a beer.

"Hey, Mama. Whoa, it smells so good in here. Did you do something with apples?" Mandy said, coming in the front door.

"Hey, baby, I did. Apple cinnamon pound cake." She had a great sense of smell. She was an excellent cook as well.

"It smells amazing."

"Want a piece?" I could spare one for my girl.

"Are you sure? I know those are for the shop."

"Yeah, it's fine." We headed to the kitchen, and I sliced us each a thick piece. She started to heat water for tea. "So, how were the kids? Are they excited to come home?"

"Yeah, they are. Missy kept talking about how she missed her bed here. They have a cute room at Jimmy's, but it isn't home for them."

The tea was ready, so we sat at the table with our slice of cake and tea. She smiled over at me. I knew just what she was thinking and smiled back. Then as if on cue, we bit into the sweet, tangy bread at the same time. This was something we had always done. One of our few traditions.

"Mmmm... this is so good. Wow. I think this is one of your best."

"Thanks, I agree." It was good. I would add this to my rotation.

We chatted, sipped tea, and ate our cake. It was a nice way to end the day. When my phone chimed, and the display flashed Ricky's name, she said good night.

Still awake?

Yes

My phone rang. "Hey, beautiful."

"Hey, handsome. How was the rest of your day?"

"Great. Yours?"

"It was good. Missy and Davy will come home tomorrow. I'm excited."

"Oh, that's good. I know you will be glad to have them home."

"Definitely."

"So, I am off Thursday. Are you?"

"I am. What are you thinking?" I asked coyly.

"I was thinking maybe you and I go to Galveston. Do some touristy things. Whatcha think?"

"I say, let's do it."

"Great!"

We finalized our plans, chatted a little more, and then said good night. I went to bed with the biggest smile and a warm heart.

The next day flew by. The bakery sold out of all of my cakes. However, there was high praise for the new apple cinnamon bread, so I knew for sure I would be adding it as one of my regulars.

As usual, I made more about halfway through the day, but we sold out of those too. All the locals would line up, and we were starting to have people drive in from other parts of the Houston area for them. They said they heard about us from friends and family.

Later that night, I was making dinner when I heard the most beautiful sound. My babies.

"Mama! Mama, I'm home!" My Missy girl.

My heart soared, and I ran out of the kitchen to meet them.

"Hey, my babies. Welcome home!" I wrapped them in my arms and kissed their cheeks. Oh, my sweet babies. "I missed you both."

"We missed you, Mama." Davy just nodded along with her and hugged me tightly.

"Thanks, Jimmy."

"My pleasure. I loved having them. Maybe we need to talk about trading weekends or something." He looked hopeful.

"Yes, I think maybe we should." I hated it, but it was only fair. He was a wonderful and involved father. "We can figure out what works for everyone."

"Davy, let's go see if our room is still the same." Missy squealed and ran towards her room.

Jimmy and I laughed. Why would they think their room was different? Cuties. I had cleaned it and washed the sheets, vacuumed, but nothing major. I heard Missy get excited. What was she seeing? I gave Jimmy an odd look and headed down the hall.

"Mama, my room is so pretty! Thank you." I looked at her, confused.

"I didn't do anything. I just cleaned it."

"I know, and it's beautiful. I love it." I hugged her. She was a funny little girl. Happy about small things.

"It doesn't look different to me." Little Davy came in with a pout.

"I cleaned it."

"You did?" He looked up at me.

"Yes. I washed your sheets, dusted everything, and vacuumed your floor."

"Really?" I nodded. He jumped to me. "Tank you, Mama. Tank you, tank you!"

I loved my children. They were so sweet and innocent. Jimmy had come in and was watching our interaction with an amused smile.

"Do you want to stay for dinner? I made spaghetti."

"That sounds good, yes, thank you." He said.

"Mandy should be home soon. I better finish cooking." I left them and headed back to the kitchen.

As I finished up dinner, sounds of them playing drifted down the hallway. Missy came in after a few minutes to join me. She chatted away as I worked. She offered to help, so I had her help me put a salad together. We laughed and made jokes as we worked.

What a fun moment. How had I missed out on this for so long? It made me think of Mandy as a little girl. Would she have been like this had I been more of a mother to her? More innocent and less serious.

As if appearing from my thoughts, Mandy came into the kitchen.

"Hey, Mama. Hey, Missy." She hugged her little sister and then kissed my cheek.

"Hi, baby. I was just thinking about you." I said.

"Oh yeah, anything good?"

"Yeah, remembering you as a little girl." I smiled at her.

She smiled back with a bit of sadness in her eyes, less sparkle in them. It reflected how I was feeling, but we also had peace there too. She knew and squeezed my hand.

"So, how does it feel to be home, Missy?" Mandy asked her.

"I'm happy! Mama cleaned my room." I couldn't believe she was still excited about that. She was hilarious.

"What a lucky girl you are," Mandy said to her.

"I helped Mama make the salad. Look!" She grabbed the bowl to show Mandy and nearly dropped it. Thank goodness she didn't. Mandy helped steady her.

"It's beautiful. Let's put it on the table. Want to help me get the table set?" She helped Missy get it settled on the table. "Is Jimmy staying for dinner? I saw his truck."

"Yes, he said he was."

"I heard my name." He put his arm around her.

"Hi, babe."

That pinch of jealousy was there, but I would see Ricky tomorrow, so it was good. I just wished I could have him here with me now to share our own intimate moment. Someone to share a touch, a look, or a laugh with that nobody else would understand. I'd never really had that, or not since Ricky and I were teens. Maybe we'd have that again.

Missy and Mandy finished getting the table set. Jimmy got little Davy cleaned up and settled at the table. Mandy served salad to the little kids so they could get started.

Jimmy and Mandy chatted about their day and whispered a little to each other. It was the type of intimate communication that couples do. I tried not to listen or watch them too much, but I couldn't help myself. It was sweet, and I got to be a witness to their love. As her Mama, it warmed my heart that she had found love.

Dinner was ready, so we joined the kids with our salads. Then after salads, we got plates of pasta and garlic bread. The kids ate so well, each eating a pile of spaghetti.

We chatted, joked, and laughed through the whole meal. It was comfortable and felt great to have our little family together.

After dinner, Jimmy and Mandy said they would clean up, so I took the kids into the backyard. This was part of the routine that Mandy had put in place for the kids. Outdoor playtime after dinner, then baths, reading time, and then bed. It had always worked really well, so we all kept it going.

I got their kickball out of the shed and played a game like the basketball game horse, just without a hoop as we didn't have one. We used the legs of the swing set, and you had to throw, kick, or roll the ball a certain way or did a trick, like a twirl, and throw it at the same time to get it in the goal. Then everyone else had to do it the same. If you missed it, you got a letter, and the first to spell horse lost. The person with the fewest letters won.

Jimmy and Mandy joined the game after a few rounds. I got tired, so I tapped out and sat on the back porch to watch for a while.

"Hello." It was our neighbor Caroline.

"Grammy!" The kids ran to greet her with a hug.

I waved, and she joined me on the porch.

"I heard y'all out here and thought I would come to visit for a few minutes." She said, taking a seat next to me.

"I'm glad you did."

"You aren't playing?"

"I was, but I got hot." I fanned myself with my hand. Unfortunately, it did little against the warm Texas humidity.

"It looks like life is getting back to normal. No more angry folks taking up space." She commented.

"Yes, I'm so glad that the press conference worked for us. That was getting really ugly. Thank you so much for your help."

The little kids decided they were done with the game and started to play on their swing set. Jimmy had gotten it for them a month or so ago. It was an excellent addition to our backyard.

Since the game broke up, Jimmy and Mandy came to join us on the porch. It was starting to get dark, and the kids needed to get baths, so Ms. Graham said good night. Mandy walked Jimmy out. I took the little kids in so they could get baths, brush their teeth, and I could read to them.

We were reading Pippi Longstocking by Astrid Lindgren. It was a favorite of mine as a child, and I thought the kids would love it. Missy has a fantastic imagination and loves adventure, so it was a perfect fit.

After the kids were tucked in, I headed to the living room to watch Chopped's latest episode. Mandy was on the computer. She was always working.

"Will the TV bother you?"

"Not at all. Go ahead." She worked for a few minutes, and before long, she had joined me.

We debated who we thought would win, discussed what they were making, and shared what we thought we would make from the mystery ingredients. Though it turns out, we were both wrong about the winner.

"So, you're going to Galveston tomorrow with dad?" Mandy asked.

I loved hearing her call him that. They had been working on a relationship and talked regularly. It was nice.

"Yes, I'm excited."

"How's Amelia doing with everything?"

"He says she is doing okay. I'm not sure yet. We're talking about going out with all the kids so they can see us together. I know he wants that mostly for Amelia, but I'm unsure."

"Yeah, she was not happy at Missy's party, but that was a month ago."

"I know. I'm worried that she will never accept me."

"I'm sure she will. Just be patient."

Her phone chimed. "Oh, it's Claire. I need to go call her. We had a schedule change. Good night." She kissed my cheek and then called Claire as she walked to her room.

I watched a few more food shows before deciding to go to bed. I had a fun day planned for tomorrow, and I wanted to be ready for it. Hopefully, my excitement didn't keep me from sleeping.

Chapter Sixteen

I stretched and checked the clock. I had managed six solid hours of sleep, which for me was good. Usually, my brain wouldn't shut down, so I would end up lying awake with my anxiety and every mistake I have ever made running nonstop through my head.

I swung out of bed with a smile, then made my way to the kitchen for coffee and to see the little kids. They were eating cereal. Mandy was in the living room on what sounded like a work call.

"Good morning, babies." I kissed them each on the head.

"Good morning, Mama." They sang.

"Did you both sleep well?" I poured some coffee into a mug and added a splash of creamer.

"I did. I had the bestest dream ever! Olive, Darla, and I were kittens. It was so funny. We got to play with kitty toys and chase mice, but we didn't catch them, just chased them." Little Davy was giggling as Missy talked about her dream.

"That's so silly, Missy. You aren't a kitty!" He was so tickled by her dream. He almost couldn't stop laughing.

"I know that, Davy. It was just a funny dream. They are for pretend." The sass was strong with this one. She knew how to use it too.

"I think it's a great dream. It might be fun to be a cat for a little while."

"Can we get a kitty?" Oh wow, I should have seen that coming.

"I don't know about getting a cat right now."

"What about a puppy?"

"I don't know if we can have a kitten or a puppy right now but maybe in the future and when you both get a little older."

They pouted slightly, but thankfully Mandy raised them to not argue. I was so thankful for her because I didn't know that I would have done quite as good a job with them. If they had asked me a few more times, I probably would have given in.

"Hey, Mama. Ready for your date?" Mandy said, smiling brightly. She had ended her call and had just joined us in the kitchen.

"I am. Looks like the weather is going to be nice too."

"You're going on a date, Mama?" Missy asked. "Do you have a boyfriend?"

"Yes, I am, and I do. Is that okay?"

"Is it Mr. Ricky? I like him, and if you get married, Darla and I will be sisters."

"It's Mr. Ricky, but baby, we aren't talking about getting married. So don't get too excited about that."

"But it could happen, right?"

"Anything is possible, but we're not close to that at all, so don't go telling people." I didn't need her telling Darla and Amelia overhearing. "Do you know what a rumor is?"

"I think so."

"Well, it's kind of like lying, so we don't want to lie, right?"

"No, Mama."

"Are you both ready to go? I have to get to work, and Mama has to get ready for her date." Mandy asked them.

"Yes, Mandy. Come on, Davy. Let's get our shoes on."

"Okay, Sissy."

They both ran off to get their shoes on. Then they both sang their way down the hall and put on their shoes.

"Have fun today, Mama. Can't wait to hear how it goes." She leaned over and kissed my cheek before grabbing her keys and purse, then yelled out for the kids to join her. They did, waving to me as they followed her out the door.

I sat there for a second, soaking in anticipation of a fun day. I would get a whole day with him, my true love. Things had been a bit crazy the past few weeks, but I was ready to enjoy the day. Butterflies started in my stomach as I thought, letting the excitement build.

"Well, better get ready," I said to nobody.

I pushed up from the table, rinsed my coffee mug before going to shower and dress. I selected a cute sleeveless tank and denim capris, then slipped on some cute but comfy sandals. Added a little mascara and lip gloss, nothing fancy, then pulled my hair up into a ponytail as it was often breezy and hot on the island.

I checked the clock. I had about ten minutes to spare before he would be here, so I checked various social media sites on my phone to see if anything was new. A few friends were posting about work.

Steph added a few new pictures of Sammy. He was getting big and starting to pull up on furniture.

She also posted about a new project they were working on at their house and were buying their first house to flip. Seeing her updates reminded me I needed to set up a lunch with her soon.

There were also a few new pictures of Mandy and Jimmy from a recent date. They were cute together, and I was happy for them both.

There was a knock on the door, causing my pulse to quicken. I took a deep breath as I stood and walked to the door.

He was wearing a plain red t shirt and khaki shorts with a ball cap, sunglasses perched on the brim.

"Good morning, beautiful."

"Good morning to you, handsome."

He leaned over and kissed me softly. Swoon.

"Ready?" He whispered.

"Yep!"

He opened the car door for me and then climbed in himself, and we were off.

"So, I thought we would head to the Strand first and then eat lunch somewhere on the Seawall. What do you think?"

"Sounds good. I was looking up some things and thought the Railroad Museum might be interesting. I remember Caroline talking about it."

"I think I have been there once. Okay, add that to our list."

The drive from Glenn Lake to Galveston was about an hour. It gave us plenty of time to talk about old times, kids, and sports. Then when a favorite song came on the radio, we sang along.

"Remember this one?"

"Yes, when you took me to my first high school dance." I remembered well. I had had to lie to my parents about it.

"You looked so beautiful in that wine colored dress."

I blushed at the memory. That night had been our first time together, and though I wasn't a virgin, it had felt so much more special with him. There was love between us, and I knew instantly our relationship was different.

When we hit the causeway, I felt my body relax. I loved coming to the island. It wasn't the prettiest place on Earth, but it was my happy place, and for many that lived in the Houston area, it was a place they headed for a weekend of fun.

We headed down Broadway and to 25th street before turning towards the Strand. We parked near the museum in a metered parking lot.

There weren't many people around this early on a weekday, so it was quiet on the street. We headed straight to the Railroad Museum, paying our admission fee, and then began our self guided walking tour. We boarded some of the old train cars, commenting on the interiors and layout of the trains.

"What do you think it was like riding in one of these?" I asked as I tested out the seat in one of the old passenger trains. The seat's fabric was worn, but the springs still had support and some bounce to them.

"Hot!" He said.

"For sure." I laughed.

We continued walking through the different train cars in various states of restoration. We contemplated the places people would travel to and their individual stories.

"Where do you think they came from?" I said as I sat in one of the restored bench seats. The fabric was mint green with gold pinstripes.

"Chicago, New Orleans, maybe all the way from Boston."

"It would have been so beautiful chugging along through the country."

We then made up a couple that would meet at the train station and run away together because their families disapproved of them. It was a kind of Romeo and Juliet with a train themed story. We were laughing and creating this wild story together. It was almost perfect.

"They were madly in love," I said.

"Nothing was going to stop them from being together."

"They both worked odd jobs to save money for the new life."

"Finally, the day came. They boarded the train and lived happily ever after in Midland, TX, with five kids."

"That's a nice ending." I smiled at him. We held hands as we strolled out of the museum.

"That was fun. I am glad we did that." He said, squeezing my hand a little.

I returned the gesture. "Me too."

We left the museum and strolled over to the Strand. It's known for its cute local retail shops, art galleries, antique stores, and many restaurants. In addition, they held festivals like Dickens on the Strand or Mardi Gras at different times throughout the year.

We went inside a few different stores, just browsing and enjoying each other's company. Then, stepping into a souvenir shop, we decided to get each of our kids something fun.

We found a small tote bag with a Galveston logo on it for Darla and Missy.

"Missy would like a pink one. What color does Darla like?" I asked him.

"She loves blue, so this one will be perfect."

We walked around browsing and found the boys an inflatable beach ball, and then he picked out an oversized t shirt for Amelia.

"She will like this for sleeping in. She likes to steal my t shirts sometimes."

"That's cute. I can picture her in daddy's shirt. I'm sure she will love this then."

"What about Mandy? Is she too old for a silly souvenir?"

"Hmm, I think she would love something. I think a t shirt for her too, maybe?"

We flipped through the shirts.

With gifts in hand, we paid and headed back to the car and then to get some lunch. We drove to the Seawall to a small fish and chips shop, where we sat on the deck overlooking the Gulf. It was the perfect day for it. We each ordered a shrimp and fish basket with fries and coleslaw.

I stared at the water. The day had been perfect. He must have been thinking it too because he reached across the table and took my hand.

"I've had a good day. Thank you." He said.

"I did too. I'm so glad you asked."

Our food arrived shortly after and was hot, crispy, and perfect. We ate and made small talk.

Too soon, it was time to head back. I had baking to do, and he had kids to pick up. The drive home was just as easy and comfortable, but underneath my smiles, I was already dreading the goodbye.

He pulled in front of the house, parked, and turned to me. He took my hand in his, squeezing it gently, then smiled. It warmed me to my soul.

"I really did have a good time today."

"Me too," I said, brushing a stray hair from my face.

"We haven't exactly talked about what we are, but I'd like to say, girlfriend. Maybe?" He gave a slight shoulder shrug and grinned like a shy twelve year old.

"What? No note with a place to check yes or no." I teased.

"Ha, ha. No, but that would have been funny."

"Yeah, but to answer, I'd love to be your girlfriend."

"Geez, I feel like an awkward teen again."

He smiled, then pulled me to him for a toe curling kiss. It wasn't the best place for making out, mostly since it was the middle of the afternoon and sitting in front of my house. Any neighbor could see us.

"We need to find some time to be alone." We had been alone all day, but I knew what he meant. I agreed. "Well, I better go before this gets too far..." One more kiss or two. "I love you, Becca."

My heart fluttered. He hadn't said those words in over eighteen years.

"I love you."

One final kiss, then he hopped out to come open my door.

"You're the sweetest. Thanks, Ricky."

He handed me my bag of souvenirs for my kids. We got to my door, where we found it hard to simply say goodbye. I wanted to invite him inside and not let him leave until morning.

Unfortunately, it was nearly time for Mandy to get home, and Jimmy would be here soon with the little kids. I had to get batters mixed for work and dinner prepped. Darn it all, being an adult sucked sometimes.

One more, okay, two more kisses, and we finally said our goodbyes. He assured me he would call later.

After he was gone, I got to work on mixing up batches of goodies for the next day. Brown butter, cinnamon pecan, and banana were the special for tomorrow. They were the favorites.

As I worked, I couldn't stop smiling about Ricky and remembering the day. It had been just what the doctor ordered. Relaxing, just the two of us, no worries.

"Well, someone looks happy." Mandy's voice startled me as I had been lost in my daydreams. "I guess you had a good day."

"Yeah, it was pretty good."

"I was never the girl to daydream about my parents getting back together. I never even thought to wish it as I didn't know him, but now... Now I know and do wish for that."

"Aww, that's sweet. I hope for that too."

We heard the front door open and then the sweet voices of my youngest two.

"Hi, Mama!" They both came around the kitchen corner and straight to me for a hug, then hugged their sister.

"We had the best day today. For show and tell, Mia brought her new puppy! She had a bow on her head, and she knew a bunch of tricks. Like, she had a little pink ball and would catch it. She was soo cute. Her name is Moxie. Can we get a puppy? Please, oh please? I will love it forever, and I will feed it and brush it and play with it. It can sleep with me too." She said all so fast and with such excitement, I hated to break her heart.

"We've talked about this. We can't get a puppy right now, sweetie. Maybe someday."

How did this topic keep coming up? As always, I knew I'd give in, but for now, I was still recovering both mentally and physically.

"But, Mama, I promise to help. Please? Please?"

"Peas, Mama!" Davy chimed in.

"Not right now, and I'm not going to argue about it. Now go put your backpacks away and then wash up for dinner."

"Yes, Mama." They walked off, heads down to do what I said. Jimmy and Mandy were trying not to laugh.

"Sorry, I told them on the way home that they were not ready for a puppy. She was not convinced and tried to talk me into one, but I said I couldn't with being gone all day."

"I know I will probably give in and get one someday but not yet."

Mandy took over dinner where I had left off, so I was able to wrap up my baking by getting everything bundled up for the next day.

There was no more talk of puppies, especially when I gave them their gifts. I knew the topic would come up again, and next time I'd probably say yes because I wanted a pet almost as much as they did. However, for once in my life, I was trying to do the right thing.

Chapter Seventeen

I finally heard from the DA that Butch would make a full recovery from his attack and would be going to trial soon. He would keep me updated as he got the exact court date, tentatively scheduled for a few weeks from now.

"Also, I need to let you know, Butch's family was finally able to bail him out." At his words, my body tensed, and I started shaking. "They hadn't tried hard to get him out, but when he was attacked, they wanted to keep him safe."

"Oh, okay, thank you for letting me know," I said. My throat tightened, and I struggled to say more.

"I'm sorry, Becca, but he does have an ankle monitor and isn't supposed to leave Harris County, so you should be good in Glenn Lake since it's outside of that."

"Thanks." I didn't feel safe, but I was going to hold on to that.

Other than that, the next few days were uneventful, and before I knew it, Sunday was here. We were swamped at the bakery all morning, but unlike most days, the clock barely moved. I swear when you have something fun planned for the day, the rest of that day feels longer than it should, and this Sunday was no different.

"Anxious?" Mary was smirking at me.

"Sorry, is it that noticeable?"

"Yeah, you keep peeking at the clock and giving a heavy sigh, but it's cute!"

"Just excited and a little nervous about meeting up with Ricky and his kids. I know it's important to him that Amelia likes me, and she doesn't. I don't blame her. She lost her mother and probably thinks I want to take her place. I couldn't even if I tried. You only have one true mother. Others can love you just as much, but your mother is... Well, your mother, right?"

"I don't think that it's completely true. I think, say, an adoptive parent can be your parent just as truly as your biological one. Many stepparents do more and love more than the other parent. Families come in all shapes and sizes."

"That's true. You're right. But I guess just thinking about how they lost her to cancer like that... I don't want to take her place, but I will be the best..." I sighed. "Whatever I am to them that I can. Does that make sense?"

She nodded her agreement and gave me a hug.

"I know what you mean, and you will be great. I hope she learns to love you."

More customers entered the store, so we both got back to work. Tick tock, tick tock. The clock was torturing me. I worked hard not to let my boss or customers know how ready I was for the workday to end.

I had left instructions and food for Mandy on what to bring to the park. The kids were extremely excited.

For days now, Missy had been talking about going to the park with one of her bestest friends in the whole wide world. Of course, I knew she would enjoy herself. But most of the kids I wasn't worried about. It was just one in particular that I had concerns over.

Finally, it was closing time. I helped Mary clean up and prep for the next day. She did try to send me on my way a few times, but I insisted that I finish the day. At two on the dot, we were locking up behind us, and I was walking as fast as I could to the park. Thankfully, it was one block over and straight ahead.

"Mama. Mama." Little Davy saw me first and came running. Mandy turned to see where he was running, and when she saw me, waved. I waved back and caught Little Davy at almost the exact moment.

"Are you having fun?"

"Yep, I playing with Tomas. He littler than me, but I like to play with him anyway."

"Oh, that's nice. I'm glad you like playing with him."

I walked over to join everyone, still holding Davy. He hugged me around the neck and then squirmed to get down, so I put him down. He was running back to the playground, and Tomas ran to meet him. They ran off together. It looked like they had dump trucks in the sandbox.

"Hi, beautiful." Ricky gave me a quick side hug. Amelia was nearby, watching closely.

"Hey. How's it going so far?"

"Good, good. Everyone has just been playing, and Mandy, Amelia, and I were sitting here visiting." He smiled at the two sisters.

They looked so much alike, even some of their mannerisms. It was amazing to watch them together.

"Do you think they are ready to eat? I can start getting it set out." I offered.

"I could eat. I'll see if the little ones are ready." He went to the playground to talk to the little kids. Mandy and I started unpacking the picnic.

Ricky returned without kids. "They aren't ready to eat. So I'm going to just let them play."

"Okay, well, we can eat." I gestured towards the food.

"It all looks good, Mama."

"Yes, thank you, Ms. Becca," Mel said softly.

"You're welcome. I hope you enjoy it."

We all helped ourselves to sandwiches, potato salad, chips, and some fruit slices. Ricky had brought some bottled water and sodas.

"Good potato salad, Mama," Mandy said.

Ricky nodded his agreement. Amelia was silent, her eyes down while she ate, only peeking occasionally at me here and there. I think she was still trying to feel me out.

We made small talk while we ate. Ricky helped himself to seconds. I cleaned up a bit, and Mandy pulled out a deck of cards. She and Amelia played a card game that Amelia had learned in school. Mandy seemed to know it already. I wondered if it was something common, or maybe she learned it in school too. Ricky and I watched them.

He caught my eye a few times and smiled at me. He would look back at the girls, and I could almost hear his thoughts as he took in the similarities between them. I was doing the same.

They had the same bone structure, high cheekbones, sharp chins. Their eyes were the same hazel, and they moved almost in sync with each other. It was almost spooky.

After a while, Davy and Tomas came to the table. I helped them get settled. I had some wet wipes to wash their hands with. Not perfect, but it would work. They were both quiet, just grinning happy little boys, and when I got the food in front of them, Davy started humming as he ate, so Tomas copied him.

While the boys ate, Ricky was dealt into the card game. The three of them laughed and chatted.

This was a moment I knew I would cherish forever. Father, mother, and children all enjoying time together. Oh, how I always wanted this exact thing.

My childhood had not been this ideal. On the outside, people probably thought we were the typical American family living the dream. But in reality, there was a lot of physical and emotional abuse. I was beaten and belittled almost daily. I never felt loved, and wasn't that what you were supposed to do with children?

Okay, so I wasn't the best example, but going from the abuse to pregnancy and kicked out to having to fight to survive with an infant and the things I had to do some days to get by, it had been too much to bear.

After losing my parents, I would get angry and frustrated, thinking I was as horrible as they said. Perhaps I did deserve to be punished, beaten, and was trashy. It was almost like I was trying to be what they thought I was.

I loved my children. I just didn't know how to love them. I was learning to let them lead me in what they needed and how to show them. Mandy had gotten the worst of me, and she was still such a kind hearted person and had raised her siblings to be like her.

She loved them with her whole heart. Over the last few months, since my accident, I have seen how much she loved the little ones, and I took most of my cues from her.

"You're looking way too seriously over there," Ricky whispered.

"Sorry, I was just taking in the moment. It's a nice moment."

"Yes, yes, it is." He looked at me so intensely, sending chills through my whole body.

Little Davy and Tomas finished up their lunches and ran back to play. As they headed back, Missy and Darla bounced over and were ready for some food. The game to my left continued hand after hand and laugh after laugh. The little girls chatted happily amongst themselves while Ricky and the older two talked. So I decided I would go play with the little boys.

When I joined them, Davy was thrilled and announced I could push them on the swing. Tomas ran to it and pointed.

"You want to swing, Tomas?"

He smiled and babbled something.

"I'll take that as a yes."

I picked him up, placed him in the baby swing, and gave him a gentle push. Davy ran to the one next to him, so I put him in and pushed. I stood between the two of them, giving a little push here and there.

"Tomas, Tomas! Look at us. We swing." Davy giggled and giggled.

"Swing, swing... Wee, wee."

I think that was the first time I really heard Tomas speak, at least words. He had either been quiet or baby babble.

They laughed and begged for more. Davy wanted to go higher, faster, higher, faster. Tomas tried to copy him.

After several minutes, movement at the picnic table caught my eye. I looked over to see Ricky packing things up and Mandy dealing another hand. The four girls were laughing together and talking with each other.

Soon Ricky joined us at the swings. He stood in front of the boys and pretended to be a monster making monster sounds and acting like he would grab them. They squealed and giggled in delight at the scary monster.

The boys tired of the swings, and the girls got restless, so Ricky put the picnic stuff in our respective cars, and we all walked over to the lake.

We walked out on the wooden pier that went out over the water. It had trails that went out in a few directions.

Glenn Lake was marshy with lots of birds, turtles, and other wildlife. Some people were fishing, and others, like us, just enjoying the scenic view and beautiful weather. This is one of the reasons people come to Glenn Lake, for the park and lake.

We walked around the lake, taking in the views and watching the kids bond. They were walking in pairs. The older girls, the little girls, and the boys. Each group chatting, having their own moment together. I sighed with contentment. Ricky and I held hands and watched them.

Soon, too soon, it was time for us all to head home. It had been a wonderful day. Full of good laughs and memories. I hoped the kids enjoyed it as much as I did. Ricky caught my eye a few times, and I could tell he felt the same.

The boys ran ahead, Tomas' little legs barely keeping up with Davy, but he tried hard. The two little girls chattered and held hands. Mandy and Amelia walked side by side, enjoying the last few moments together for today. They reminisced about their card game and made plans to get together just the two of them soon.

The look on Amelia's face told me she looked up to her older sister. I knew she wasn't happy about me, but she seemed to be enjoying having a big sister. She had almost a "my hero" look as she beamed up at her older sister.

As we reached the cars, I was feeling a slight dread of saying goodbye to this day. By the looks on everyone's faces, I guessed they felt the same.

We started our goodbyes. Darla hugged me and said it was the best day ever. I guessed Missy wasn't the only intense and theatrical five-year-old. No wonder she, Olive, and Missy were all friends.Tomas threw himself at me. "Bye, Mama."

Everyone gasped. My heart fluttered, then dropped. It was like being slapped.

My eyes went instantly to Amelia. She looked like one of those cartoon characters with steam coming out of her ears. Her face was red, and her nostrils flared as she looked at me.

"You!... You! I knew it. You want to replace my mom." Tears started streaming down her face. "You will *NEVER* be my mother. I hate you! I hate you! I hate you!" She ran off.

"Amelia...!" But she was gone. Ricky's shoulders sank as he watched her go, but he didn't make a move to go after her.

"I will get her." Mandy took off after her.

"I'm so sorry. I'm so sorry. I didn't..." I was near tears myself.

Darla and Missy looked so confused.

"No, I'm sorry. She doesn't understand."

We just stood there waiting. Mandy finally caught up to Amelia. They were too far away to hear what was said, but it looked like a heated conversation. Amelia was yelling, crying, and gesturing wildly. Mandy's body language was calm as she spoke to her little sister.

The rest of us didn't speak, but Tomas started getting whiny and sleepy, so Ricky turned on his car and put Tomas in the car seat. Tomas settled right in for a nap. The other kids started getting anxious too.

"Is Amelia going to be okay?" Darla took her father's hand.

"She will, but we need to be patient with her."

The worry on his face hurt my heart. He looked like he had aged ten years in that moment. I wanted to hug him, but I really didn't want to make things worse.

Finally, Mandy was guiding Amelia back to the cars. Amelia's face was still red, her eyes puffy from crying. She didn't really look up as they got closer.

"Amelia, I'm sorry I..." I tried.

"Don't speak to me. I don't like you. I will never like you. You're nothing to me but especially not my mother." She continued past us and climbed into her father's car.

I didn't want to replace her mother, but yet her words stung.

"I tried. She's very upset. I mean, obviously." Mandy had tears in her eyes.

"It's okay. I know you tried. Thank you." Ricky hugged her quickly, got Darla into the car, and then turned towards me. "I don't know what to say or do, but... I will try to call you later. It had been a great day." He climbed into his car without hugging or kissing me, barely even a second look.

This was painful for him. He was as heartbroken as I was that Amelia couldn't accept me. Was there always going to be drama with her? Would any outing we tried to have end in tears?

Mandy and I got Missy and Davy into our car to head home. I didn't know what was happening with Ricky and Amelia. I didn't know what the future of our relationship would be, but all I knew was what just happened couldn't be good.

Chapter Eighteen

We got home from the park. Mandy unloaded the car while I put little Davy to bed. He had fallen asleep almost as soon as we left the park. I laid him in bed and kissed his head.

I was so happy that I wasn't missing out on this part of his life like I had with my girls. I watched him breathe as he slept so peacefully. He was so sweet.

I closed his door and walked into the living room. Mandy was on the computer, and Missy had a coloring book on the floor. I got down next to her to admire her picture. She beamed proudly.

"That's beautiful, baby. I love all the colors you used."

"Thank you, Mama. I love, love, love to color. I try to stay in the lines, but sometimes I get outside of them. Ms. Belinda says that's okay because art is about expressing yourself, not being perfect."

"Ms. Belinda is very smart. What are you coloring?"

"It's a mermaid. See her tail? I made it purple and pink because those are my favorite colors. And her hair is yellow like mine used to be before it got darker."

"It's gorgeous. You're quite the artist."

"Do you want to color? I have another book." She jumped up, not waiting for me to answer, and grabbed another one from a shelf in the living room. Mandy had made a nice place for the kids to have art and crafts supplies.

Missy presented the book to me and then plopped down on the floor again. "This one has animals. You can do the elephant. Elephants are gray, but you can make yours any color you want because it's your art."

"Maybe I'll make a purple elephant."

"Ooh, that would be so pretty! Purple elephants are probably the prettiest kind."

We colored for a while together. Spending this time with her was fun. We chatted as we colored about her favorite animals, her friends at school, and which crayons were the best ones. She was an interesting and complicated little person who thought of things very deeply.

"Mama, I'm sorry about what happened at the park. I know you are worried about it, but I think it will all work out fine." Missy said after some time. Oh, melt my heart.

"I hope so, baby." I kissed her head. "How did you get to be so wise?"

"I don't know. I just think about things a lot. Mandy says I'm an old soul." She carefully selected a blue crayon and began coloring the sky in her picture. "Mama, do you think Amelia will ever like you?"

The question caught me off guard. "I don't know, sweetheart. She's been through a lot. She lost her mommy, and that's really hard."

"I would be so sad if I lost you." Missy set down her crayon and looked at me with those big eyes. "But I don't think I would be mean to people."

"Everyone handles sadness differently. We just have to be patient with her."

Missy nodded thoughtfully. "I'll be extra nice to her. Maybe that will help."

"That's very kind of you, baby."

She picked up her crayon again and worked quietly for a moment. "Are you done coloring, Mama? I think I'm going to play with my dolls now. They've been waiting for me all day, and I promised them we would have a tea party."

"I'm done. Thank you for sharing your coloring books with me. I had fun."

"You're welcome. Your purple elephant turned out really good. You should put it on the fridge."

"Maybe I will."

She gathered up her crayons carefully, putting each one back in the box in its proper spot. "Mama, you can color with me anytime you want. I like it when you do things with me."

"I like it too, sweetheart. More than you know."

I helped her clean up the coloring books, and she ran off to play. I sat back and watched Mandy on the computer.

Truth be told, I was worried about Ricky. I hadn't heard from him yet. He would pick his children over me. That was okay. I would be upset, distraught even, but children come first. They have to. I had learned, but a few months ago, I wouldn't have been so understanding. Nearly dying in a car accident makes you realize what is most important in life and what really isn't.

Missy's words echoed in my head. "I like it when you do things with me." Such a simple thing, coloring together on the floor, and yet it meant so much to her. To both of us. These were the moments I had missed with Mandy, the quiet everyday moments that build a childhood. I was grateful I wasn't missing them anymore. She was such a hard worker. She had recently hired a third employee and was currently going over bills, scheduling, and writing out paychecks.

I was kind of lost at the moment. I didn't have to bake tonight because tomorrow Mary's bakery was closed as it was Monday. I did have a counseling session tomorrow, and I wasn't looking forward to it. I also had an AA meeting in the evening.

"You okay, Mama?" Mandy was looking at me with concern.

"I'm okay. Just thinking about my to do list for tomorrow."

"Ms. Graham is watching the kids tomorrow, right?"

The daycare had a school holiday as they had a staff training day planned. They had them twice a year to ensure that the staff had time for recertification.

"Yes. She's wonderful, and I know the kids will have fun with her."

We chatted a bit about nothing really, and thankfully neither of us brought up the incident at the park. After a while, she got back to her emails, and I sat there looking around.

My body hummed with nervous energy, so I got up and just wandered from room to room, looking for any distraction. My mind tried hard not to think of Ricky and what was possibly going on across town.

Between Mandy and I, the house was nearly spotless. No stray socks, shoes, or toys. No dusty shelves, no dishes to wash.

With nothing else to do, I settled in front of the television and didn't even bother to search. Instead, I put it right on Food Network. Little Davy woke up and climbed up in my lap for some snuggle time. We watched Chopped, and he loved the host and would giggle and point to him whenever they showed him.

"You chopped!" Little Davy mimicked as the first contestant was let go from the show. He continued to mimic and giggle. It was contagious, and I soon joined him with my own laughter at his "You chopped!"

"Y'all are crazy," Mandy commented from the desk.

"Mandy, you chopped!" He laughed at his own joke.

"Thanks a lot, Little Davy. I thought you liked my food." She came over and tickled him.

"I do like your food, but you still chopped." He grinned at her, so proud of himself. He was a serious little boy usually, but this silly side of him was fun to see.

His laughing got Missy's attention, and she soon joined us. It became a silly, laughing, tickle fight in our living room. It was a good distraction for me, so I didn't think about Ricky. I loved playing and having fun with the kids. For probably the millionth time since my accident, I chastised myself a little for missing all of this for way too long.

However, once the tickle fight was over and everyone was settled down, my brain immediately clicked to the thought of Ricky. I checked the time. We had been home for a couple of hours now. What was going on with Ricky? I hoped Amelia was calmer and wouldn't sway Ricky to end things. I knew it was possible, but I just had to hope.

I went to the kitchen to start dinner. We had a late lunch, so I was just going to do something light, deciding on scrambled eggs and toast for dinner. We had some leftover fruit from lunch, so I would serve that on the side.

The text notification on my phone chimed. My brain screamed, Ricky. I grabbed the phone to see it was Steph asking about lunch.

Want to get lunch soon?
Yes, maybe Thursday?
That works. Big Ron's?
Heck yes, club sandwich.
Miss you, friend.
Miss you too. See you Thursday.

That settled, I got back to making dinner, and once it was ready, I called them to the table.

"Dinner," I yelled.

Maybe if I kept my life feeling right and normal, it would stay that way. Hopefully, Ricky would call to give me good news later.

The kids came to the table.

"Eggs are my favorite. I love them for breakfast or dinner. Thank you, Mama!" Missy said.

"Me too. Me too!" Davy agreed.

The little kids chatted on and on during dinner about one thing or another. They were excited to go spend the day with their Grammy tomorrow. She didn't have her own kids, but she loved mine as if they were her own. I was lucky to have her look out for Mandy all those years and help with my younger two.

After dinner, Mandy took the little kids outside to play while I cleaned up the dinner dishes.

I kept anxiously checking my phone, and as each minute passed without a text or call. Tears pricked my eyes. A lump formed in my throat. Would he call? Would he end things? I had to prepare my mind and my heart for the worst. I knew it was coming.

I looked around the kitchen. I wished I had a beer just to take the edge off. I was feeling so flighty, like a caged bird. Was this feeling of wanting a drink ever going to go away?

I felt okay and normal most of the time, but as soon as I got a little stressed, worried, and anxious, my body would hum, and the need for a drink echoed in my head. Basically, if I was living life and one little thing didn't go right, like now, my body would scream for the relief only alcohol could bring me.

I hadn't had to call my sponsor, Rachel, yet, but with all that was happening lately between the trial, the protestors, and now Ricky, I wasn't sure how much longer I could resist the urges. I was trying.

To date, I hadn't put myself in positions to be tempted either, as I really wanted to make this work. This was the longest I had gone without a drink, and I was proud of myself. Nearly five months and counting.

"I can't believe Tomas called me Mama," I muttered.

It would have been fine. I would have corrected him and laughed it off, except he said it in front of Amelia, who was not my biggest fan. Otherwise, things wouldn't feel like they were falling apart, and I would be fine.

After I cleaned the kitchen, I joined the kids in the backyard. They were playing some game that Missy made up. She was so creative, always making up games for them to play. Sometimes it was just role playing like she might be a princess and Davy would be a dragon, a troll, a prince, and they would go on adventures to far off lands, all in the safety of our backyard. I loved to watch them.

I joined the game. We were traveling on safari, and I was supposed to be a monkey. So I did my part by hanging out on a low branch of our tree and making monkey sounds. Little Davy laughed at me to the point he ended up with hiccups, which made him laugh harder.

The game wrapped up at this point because Davy was getting too silly to continue. I got them inside, Mandy went to work on the computer, and I got the little ones into the tub.

Little Davy first because I had to help him wash and get dressed. While Missy could do most of that herself, she just needed a little supervision, mostly with her hair.

After they were dressed, we got their teeth brushed and went to their room to read.

Missy did most of the reading these days. I loved listening to her. She was an avid, strong reader. Mandy had taught her young. She was a smart little girl. I was so proud of her, all of my kids, actually.

We read a few chapters, and then it was time for bed. The little kids said good night to each other.

"Good night, sweet boy. Have sweet dreams." I kissed his head.

"Night, Mama, sweep dreams!" He yawned and snuggled his stuffed tiger that Jimmy had gotten him last time they were at the zoo.

"Time for bed, Missy girl."

"Okay, Mama. I just need to pick who is sleeping with me tonight. I slept with Pineapple last night, and I was thinking maybe Philly tonight, but I was asking them." Pineapple was a stuffed cat, and Philly was a zebra.

"That's fair."

She nodded, signaling she had decided. She grabbed them both and climbed into bed. Okay, I didn't know that was an option but okay.

I tucked her blankets in around her, Pineapple and Philly, kissed them each on their heads, and wished them a good night. She snuggled down and told me good night, adding that Pineapple and Philly said good night too.

I left their room with a smile on my face. What a fun age. Could she just stay little forever?

I walked out to the living room. Mandy was working away on the computer. I never knew what she was working on. Typically, she would answer customer emails, make the schedule for her employees, and pay bills. She had a great business going. Whenever I thought about it, it just blew my mind.

I sat and watched her work for a moment. She didn't look up for several minutes.

"How was the story tonight?" She finally said, looking over at me.

"It was good. Missy read all three chapters by herself."

"Wow. She seems to be getting more fluid with her reading. I think she's ready for kindergarten in the fall."

"Wow, hard to believe she is ready for that. It goes so fast."

"I guess no word from dad." She caught me looking at my phone.

"No, I haven't heard a thing. I'm a little worried that he will end things because Amelia will ask him. I mean, I understand. I haven't always picked you kids when I should have, so I would understand if he does. He's a good guy and wouldn't want to hurt his kids."

"He wouldn't want to hurt you either. If he did that, it would only be because of Amelia. But..." She didn't finish her thought. There really wasn't anything to say at this point, not until I knew.

"I know."

"So why don't you text him?"

"I guess I'm afraid of the answer. Plus, I know he has to care for the kids by himself. So he is probably getting them all tucked in." I looked at my phone again, knowing I wouldn't see a new message, but I looked at it anyway.

"Well, I'm sure he will message you soon." She walked over and sat on the couch next to me, leaning her head over on to my shoulder.

We sat like that for a few minutes, just enjoying each other's company. No words necessary. Her phone chimed a text.

"Oh, that's Jimmy. I'm going to go talk to him. Will you be okay?"

"I'll be fine." I lied because I definitely didn't feel fine. I needed to hear from Ricky, or I needed a drink.

"Well, good night, Mama." She kissed my head and headed to her room.

I continued to sit in the quiet living room. No television on, just sitting and listening to the silence, waiting. Finally, my phone chimed.

Hi, still awake?

Finally, a text from Ricky.

Yes

My phone rang.

"Hi."

"Hi, Becca. Sorry it took me so long to call. You can imagine things were a bit dramatic around here. I finally got things calm." My heart was beating out of my chest. I didn't want to hear how he had to calm things. Did he have to promise he wouldn't see me any longer?

"I'm glad things calmed down. I'm sorry to be the cause of so much drama... I... I didn't think I had done anything to provoke him to call me Mama."

"No, I know. Of course. He's just a little boy who heard yours calling you that and didn't know better. Amelia..." He sighed. "Amelia just needs to understand, but right now she doesn't and... Becca, this is so hard for me, but I don't think I can see you anymore. Maybe someday. Maybe when Amelia is older and healed from losing her mother."

Tears formed in my eyes. A lump swelled in my throat. I knew it was coming, but nothing could have prepared me for how I would feel to actually hear him say the words.

He continued. "Right now, though, the only thing that she asks is that I stop seeing you. I don't know what else to do. She's heartbroken still over her mother, and she doesn't understand. So, I have to do what is best for my children right now. I mean, you understand that, right?"

"Umm, oh uh, yeah, of course I understand." My heart broke. I couldn't breathe, and I had to remind my lungs to inhale, exhale. Focus.

"Becca, I'm sorry. I wish I weren't doing this over the phone. I would rather do it in person, but I can't leave the kids. I'm sorry. I love you, Becca. I will always love you. I just hope someday..." I heard him sigh. "Someday, we truly get our chance. I'm just... I'm sorry. I need to go. Bye." His voice cracked, and he ended the call without waiting for my reply.

I knew he was hurting too. Tears slowly streamed down my face. Big, huge tears. Oh, my heart. My one true love. I sat there, letting them fall. I knew he was going to end things, but I was still not prepared for this. I slowly stood and went to my room.

When I saw my bed, I collapsed into a mess of sobs and heartache. I let it all bubble up. Ricky. My Ricky. I broke his heart the first time. This time it was his turn. Of course, it didn't sound like he was faring much better than I was. He was hurting too. Much like I was nineteen years ago.

Back then, when we ended things, I cried for weeks, and again after he left town for college. It was for the best. At least that's what I'd told myself then, and he was doing it for almost the same reason now.

My decision wasn't the best, and I didn't believe his was either, but that wasn't the point. I felt mine was then, and he thought his was now. I had to respect that, even if it hurt.

I wanted to be mad at someone, but I couldn't be mad at a little broken hearted little girl. I hadn't lost my parents as young as she was, and I certainly didn't have a great relationship with them at all.

Still, I knew what that loss felt like, and I could only imagine it would have been worse if I had felt loved by them. I was almost glad when my dad passed. He was evil. My mother was just strict, but she was never as cruel as my father. Had I only done all the things they wanted, would they have loved me? Would I have been hit daily? I will never know.

God, all the pain was coming. Wave after wave of feelings and memories. As each thought, feeling, and memory hit me, the tears fell more and more. I was nearly hyperventilating.

Sleep was going to be hard to come by tonight, and I was thankful I didn't have to work or get up early. But at least I had counseling, and that would help.

I guess I fell asleep because the next thing I remember is waking to the clock showing three am. My eyes felt like they had been rubbed with sandpaper, and I had a mild headache. I got up and headed to the bathroom. I wanted to wash my face.

The mirror showed just how miserable I was. My eyes were puffy, and my face was blotchy from crying.

"Blah."

I splashed cold water on my face. The cool water felt good on my sore eyes. I stared at myself for a few seconds before turning off the light and heading back to bed.

After I was back in my room, I lay in bed, staring at the ceiling. Tomorrow I had counseling and needed to run by the DA's office. I had to get myself together so I could face those two things.

I tossed and turned the rest of the night, or I guess early morning. It was almost painful to wake up when it was finally time. My counseling session was scheduled for nine am. It was six. I had to get the little kids ready and over to Caroline's. Then drive to my appointment.

I showered and dressed before waking the kids, but they were awake. Mandy woke them and got them dressed for me. Lifesaver.

"Good morning, Mama!" They chimed when I stepped into the kitchen.

"Good morning, babies." I kissed each of their heads. Mandy had her back to me, but when she turned, she gasped slightly.

"Rough night?"

"You could say that."

"Did he call?" Mandy whispered.

"Yes... and ended things." The words opened that deep ache in my heart all over again.

"Oh, Mama, I'm sorry. Do you want me to stay with you today?"

"No, no, it's fine. I'll be fine. At least I already have my counseling scheduled today." I tried to smile. I hoped she didn't see through it.

She knew me better than that. Her arms were around me before I knew what had happened.

"I'm sorry, Mama. Call me if you need to talk." She kissed my head before releasing me. "I have to get to work. I have a full day, but I can reschedule or have the other girls take mine. Just say the word."

"I'm fine. Well, I'll be fine." The tears were right there, pressing against my eyes. But I held them back. I had to. I couldn't let Missy and little Davy see me cry. Thankfully, they were too into their cartoons to notice what we were talking about behind them.

Mandy said goodbye to the little kids and let me know that she was there for me and loved me. Then she was gone. She worked hard, but I knew she would have dropped everything for me. It wasn't worth it. There was nothing she could do, and I'd be okay. Maybe not at the moment, but with time.

"Okay, babies, finish up your breakfast, and then we need to brush teeth."

Once they were ready, I got them over to their Grammy, and I was on my way to counseling. I was not feeling it today, but I had to go. Let's just hope that I felt better after talking it out.

An hour later, I cried my eyes out in my therapist's office and talked about how much my parents let me down and how everyone except my daughter had let me down.

That wasn't wholly true, but at the moment, it felt that way. But in my heart, I knew I had Steph, Caroline, and Mary, plus many others in town.

"Am I just the type of person that is treated this way? Will I never be able to count on anyone to be there for me?" I sniffed and wiped my eyes with my fifth tissue.

"No, you deserve to be treated better. To be loved and cherished. Unfortunately, I think you are drawn to people that just let you down. Because your parents treated you that way, it set up the foundation for all other relationships in your life. You have had a few that seem positive, but overall, you're left hurt and alone. No, you don't deserve that."

"Then, why? Why am I always treated like this? Why didn't my parents love me?" Tears poured from my eyes. This sucked. I knew therapy would get me to this point, but I wanted to get through it and be on the other side.

"I can't answer that. It is possible that your parents were treated similarly and thought it was normal. Maybe they brought out the worst in each other and took it out on you. Not knowing them, I'm only guessing." She looked at her clock. "Unfortunately, time is up for today. I'm sorry. You will get through this. You're a fighter, and you have Mandy. She sounds like she supports you. That is a lot."

That was it. Another counseling session in the books. I made my next appointment and then left feeling raw. I was sure each person I passed could see my emotional baggage. I wanted to run and hide from everyone and everything.

Unfortunately, I had to head downtown to meet with the DA. They were ready to schedule Butch's trial and needed me to sign some papers for the additional charges against him for assaulting and kidnapping me. I was hoping I wouldn't have to see him. The thought scared me to my core. Our last encounter left my life changed forever. In a way, I was thankful for the second chance, but I did not want to face that again.

I got to the courthouse and walked in. I was walking down a hallway when an office door in front of me opened and out stepped Butch. My nightmare.

I wished he would have stayed in jail. How had his family been able to get that kind of money for his bail? They were all as horrible as he was.

We were alone. I looked around for an escape, nothing. I took a deep breath and continued on my journey.

"Well, well, well. Looky who it is. The bitch that threw me under the bus." I tried to ignore him and keep walking, but he followed me. Why was this hall so empty? Where were all the people? "Just going to ignore me. That's fine. I have a lot to say to you."

"Butch, please. Just leave me alone." Where was an officer when you needed them? I couldn't remember a time being in this part of the courthouse and not seeing one.

He grabbed my arm to make me stop. When I tried to pull away, he tightened his grip and whispered words meant only for me.

"Now you listen to me. You wanted everything you got, and you deserved it." He was referring to the beatings I had endured. "And you're just as responsible for those people as I am. You should be on trial with me."

"No, I was not driving, and I didn't even want to be in that car. I would have taken a cab home. We had broken up."

"You broke up, but I didn't. You were my woman." He had backed me up against a wall. Towering over me, he was now holding both of my arms. "You're still my woman. Do you hear me? And I will have you with me one way or another."

Thankfully, an officer stepped into the hall, saw how he was holding me, and approached us.

"Please let her go, sir. Are you okay, ma'am?"

"Yes, fine. I'm fine." But I wasn't. I was visibly shaking and about at my breaking point. Alcohol. I needed alcohol now.

"Sir, I am going to have to ask you to leave."

"Fine, but Becca, this isn't over." Then he was gone.

"Are you sure you are okay? Was he threatening you?"

"No, we just had some unfinished business to talk about. I'm fine. Thank you, officer."

I walked as calmly as I could. I signed the papers with the DA, speaking only briefly with the receptionist, and then left. But first, I made a quick stop in the ladies room to pull myself together. I needed to give Butch time to get away from the building before I walked out.

As I exited the building, I watched all around to make sure he wasn't close by. I walked as swiftly but calmly as I could.

Finally, I made it to my car. I couldn't take it anymore. I stopped at a liquor store before heading back to Glenn Lake. I walked the aisles like a lioness stalking her prey, but I knew what I wanted. I knew just what would kill this pain.

I bought one bottle of vodka. Okay, two. I stashed them under some things in my trunk and then headed to Ms. Graham's to pick up my babies. I told myself they were there just in case, like a security blanket. I wouldn't drink it. I wouldn't. I almost promised myself I wouldn't.

I got home and headed to get the kids from Caroline.

"Knock, knock..." She had an open door policy, but I rarely just walked in. I only did if my kids were already with her. Otherwise, I knocked and waited for her to answer.

"Hello, dear. We're just looking at old pictures."

"Oh, well, that's fun. Anything good in there?"

"Oh yes, Mama, we saw a bunch of Grammy, and did you know she lived in New York City?" Missy asked.

"I did know that, actually."

"She wanted a change of scenery, so she moved here." Missy said it with such seriousness, clearly repeating exactly what Caroline had told her. "Whatever that means."

Caroline and I shared an amused look over Missy's head, both trying not to laugh.

"It means she wanted to live somewhere different," I explained.

"Well, why didn't she just say that?" Missy shrugged. "Grown ups use such funny words sometimes."

"We are lucky she did so she can be part of our family."

"Yeah..."

"Oh, well, dear, I feel like the lucky one." Caroline said. "Let me see. I think I might have some pictures of you around here somewhere."

"Oh gosh, nobody wants to see those! Do you?" I smiled down at the kids. They looked excited to see those.

"I do! I do!"

"Me too, Mama, me too!" Little Davy bounced around and clapped.

We dug through some of the pictures until she found the ones she was looking for.

"Here we go. You are about Davy's age here."

"Oh Mama, you look so, so cute. Look at your curly hair! Just like mine!" Missy touched her curls.

"Mama, is dat you?"

"Yes, that's me, sweetie. I was about your age in this picture. Wow, I didn't realize how much he favors me. I always thought he looked more like Jimmy." I had to look at myself for a minute and then at Davy. Wow.

We continued looking at pictures with her. A shadow crossed her face as she paused on a picture of a young man in uniform.

I didn't want to make her feel bad, and I wasn't emotionally strong enough to be there for her if she was. I was a hot mess right now and felt edgy. Any little thing could set me off. If she cried, I would be a goner for sure, and those two bottles of vodka would likely be goners. Knowing they were out there made me calmer, though. Relief was just a few steps away.

"Well, we better head home. Let me help you clean these up before we go." I started to stack up pictures to put back in their boxes.

"Oh, don't worry about it, dear. I'm going to look through them for a while longer."

"Okay. Thanks for watching them."

"Anytime, anytime. I love having them." She smiled at them both.

"Thank you, Grammy!" Missy hugged her, and little Davy followed suit.

When we got home, I started working on dinner, and the little kids went to play in their room. I was still feeling antsy from my encounter with Butch. What if he made good on his threats? Would the kids be in danger too? I couldn't risk that.

I tried to work on dinner without thinking about Butch, the trial, or Ricky. I had to make my quick breads for work tomorrow too, so I needed to get dinner made for the kids.

"Hi, Mama. How was your day?" I jumped. "I'm sorry. Did I scare you?"

"Yes, hi, sorry. A little jumpy today." I sighed. "I ran into Butch at the courthouse."

"Oh, wow, how was that?"

"He threatened me. Scared the crap out of me, actually, but he is all hot air." I hoped.

"Are you sure? Maybe you should call Sheriff Riley."

"If I hear anything from him, I will. Oh, and when I picked up the kids, Caroline seemed a little... off? They had been looking at pictures. I know she doesn't talk about it, but I think there are some ghosts or sadness in her past. I know her mom is one, but... Well, I thought you might want to check on her. You have a special bond with her."

"Thanks, yeah, I'll go check on her as long as you are going to be okay, yes?"

"Yeah, baby, I'm fine. Just a little shaken, but I'm a survivor." Maybe if I said it with enough confidence, even I would believe it.

"If you are sure you are okay." She looked at me. "I'll only be a few minutes or so. I just want to make sure she is okay too."

I was mildly concerned about Caroline. I didn't know much about her past, though I knew she lost her mother to breast cancer. I think she had been engaged at one point, but I'm not sure what happened. She never married or had kids.

I finished making dinner, got the table set, and called the little kids to wash up and come to the table. Mandy got home just in time and let me know Caroline was doing better. She told me that she would fill me in later on the details, not wanting to talk in front of the little kids. Good because I wasn't sure if it would be good or bad. Either way, I felt my sanity hanging by a thread.

I kept replaying the look in Butch's eyes, and it honestly shook me to the core. I wanted to believe he was full of it, but honestly, I had felt his wrath before, plenty of times. I trembled at the memory.

Mandy gave me a look but didn't say anything. I was thankful the little kids were here to distract and keep me from answering any tough questions. Was I okay? I didn't think I was.

I really felt like I was standing on this side of sanity, trying to decide if being sane was worth it. I honestly was questioning that right now. Sanity and sobriety were both overrated. At least right now, that's how I felt.

Missy chatted away about this and that. Apparently, preschool was a dramatic place. She was always full of stories about her friends and teachers. She seemed to enjoy it, and I was glad. Mandy wasn't able to go to preschool at her age. I couldn't afford it back then. Jimmy pays for most of it now.

I smiled at Missy. I don't know what she said, but she seemed like she was waiting for my reaction. She seemed satisfied with my response and continued her story. I had to focus on my child versus my internal turmoil. She deserved my attention. My own pity party deserved none. I could spiral out of control once they were in bed.

"And then Olive said boys are stupid. She got in trouble because we aren't supposed to say stupid. She pouted while she sat in time out. Well, Joey was being mean, so I know why she said that, but you can't say stupid." Oh, if life was so simple.

"That's right, we don't call people stupid."

"Don't say stoopid. Don't say stoopid." Little Davy repeated.

"I don't say it, but Olive does all the time. She gets in trouble. You would think she would learn, but oh no, she keeps doing it." She continued to tell a new story of another girl in her class that I didn't know well. I just listened to her and replied when required.

Soon dinner was over, the kitchen cleaned, and the kids tucked in bed. Mandy was on the computer working, and I had my last batch of bread in the oven for work tomorrow. The house phone rang. Almost nobody called it. I wasn't even sure why we still had it.

"I'll get it, Mandy. Hello?"

"I told you I would find you." It was Butch.

"Butch... please, I don't have anything to say to you." I started to hang up, but before I could, he spoke.

"If I can find your phone number, don't you think I can find your house too?" There was a flash of lights in the front yard. Oh no. I crept to the window and peeked out through the slots in the blinds, careful not to move them so he wouldn't see the movement. Mandy watched me, her eyes big, but she didn't move.

"What do you want?"

"I want you to stop lying. You were just as responsible for those people as I was." I listened to him ramble on about this while I walked over to Mandy. I wrote for her to call Sheriff Riley and tell him Butch was out front.

"Butch, I think you should leave. You know I didn't want to be there with you. I had broken up with you and shouldn't have been in that car with you." I could faintly hear Mandy talking in the other room. She must be talking with Sandra, the dispatcher.

"You stupid bitch." I heard a car door, and then there was a banging on our door. "Becca, you open this door up! Right now."

"Butch, you need to leave. You will wake my children, and they aren't part of this." I tried so hard to keep my voice calm.

"Mama?" Mandy looked terrified. I was too. Where were the cops? It was taking them forever to get here. What if he got in? I couldn't even think that way. I had to be calm for Mandy.

Butch kept shouting obscenities and how he was going to kill me. Mandy and I just stood there looking at each other. Finally, the sirens. It sounded like maybe two cars coming.

"You stupid bitch. Whore! You called the cops on me. I will kill you!" He was kicking at the door. One more kick and he would likely be in.

"Butch Stevens, step away from the door with your hands up." Sheriff Riley could be heard through a bullhorn.

Muffled voices from the other side of the door.

There was a knock.

"It's Sheriff Riley. It is safe to open." His voice was unmistakable.

I hesitated, looking once to Mandy for support before opening the door. The deputies were putting Butch into the back of one of the cars. There were actually three police cars here.

"You ladies okay?"

"Yes. Thank you, Sheriff." Mandy nodded her head next to me.

"He damaged the door. We can fix this for you so it is secure for the night, but you will likely have to have the entire door replaced."

"Yes, thank you."

"I called Jimmy. He's on the way over. He can fix it." Mandy added.

"Okay, well, I'll wait until he gets here just to be safe."

"Thank you."

"Sheriff, I called for a tow truck for his car. Eddie and I are going to take him in now. You good?" One of his deputies had walked over with the update. I didn't know him. He was new, young.

"Thanks, Deputy. I'll be a few minutes behind. I'm going to get a few pictures of the door." He pulled out his phone and snapped a few pictures.

Several neighbors came out of their homes to see what was going on. Caroline came over. We filled her in, and she hugged us both. Jimmy arrived and spoke with Sheriff Riley for a moment, then joined us on the porch. Mandy rushed to him. He hugged her tight and whispered some words of comfort.

"You okay, Becca?"

"Yes. Thanks for coming."

"I see he did a number on the door. Thank goodness for solid wood doors. They don't make them quite like this anymore." He started inspecting the door to see what he would need to do to repair it.

The Sheriff stuck around until the tow truck arrived. Steve Matson was the owner of the mechanic shop and had the only tow truck in town. He would tow it over to the Sheriff's office. They had a small lot they could lock cars up in.

I watched as Steve got the car hooked up. We had gone to school together. We weren't friends but just knew each other. His dad had been the mechanic, and when Steve had graduated from school and technical school, he joined him and took over last year when his dad retired. Mr. Matson still hangs out and works from time to time when Mrs. Matson gets fed up with him at home.

Steve waved to me before leaving with Butch's car.

I turned to see Jimmy working on the damaged door frame. If Sheriff Riley hadn't been so quick to arrive, Butch might have gotten in.

I heard a slight sound from the house. Missy had been woken up by the noise. I hoped it was just Jimmy's hammering that woke her and not Butch.

"Mama, what happened? I heard a lot of noise." I scooped her up and rocked her in my arms.

"Nothing, baby, nothing to worry about. Daddy is going to fix everything." I walked her back to her room. I kissed her head and reassured her. "Daddy won't be making noise much longer. Try to ignore it and sleep."

"Okay, Mama." She was already getting sleepy again. She yawned and snuggled into her blankets.

I walked back to the front of the house. Most of the neighbors had gone back into their homes. Mandy was still talking with Caroline, so I joined them on the lawn while Jimmy finished fixing the door frame.

"Are you okay?" Mandy took my hand.

"Yeah, I think so." I didn't feel okay, but I didn't want to worry her. My mind was thinking of the vodka in my car. Oh, how that would help calm me.

This all felt surreal to me right now and couldn't have possibly happened. I would wake and discover it had all been a dream. I tried to focus on waking up, but it didn't work, so this must be a reality.

Jimmy signaled that he was finished. Caroline wished us goodnight and went home. Jimmy stayed with Mandy a few minutes. I assumed comforting her and talking about things couples talk about when there is a scary moment.

I walked back into the house to give them privacy. My mind was spinning. What a day. What was that smell?

"Oh, crap, my cake!" I ran to the oven. I pulled out the ruined cakes and practically threw them on the counter. "Well, crap, crap, crap..."

I needed to start over. I wouldn't have been able to sleep anyway. I might as well have something to do. So I pulled out ingredients and got to work.

While the cakes baked, I paced around. All I could think about was that vodka in my car. One little drink couldn't hurt. I could control it, and it would calm my nerves.

But God, this evening was scary. What if he had gotten in the house before Sheriff Riley got here? What if he had gotten my children?

I went out to the car, opened the trunk, and picked up one of the bottles. I rolled it around in my hand from one to the other, looking at it from every angle. I set it back in the car and started to close the trunk but stopped just before the click. I opened it, grabbed the bottle quickly, and then practically ran into the house.

Chapter Nineteen

I stood in the kitchen, the bottle of vodka in my hand. The house was quiet. Mandy had gone to bed. The kids were asleep. The ruined cakes sat on the counter, filling the room with the smell of burnt sugar.

My hands were still shaking from Butch's attack. Every time I closed my eyes, I pictured his face, hear him kicking at the door, screaming that he would kill me. What if Sheriff Riley hadn't gotten there in time? What if he had gotten to my children?

I just needed something to calm my nerves. Just one drink. I had earned it after the night I'd had. After the week I'd had. Ricky breaking up with me, Butch threatening me at the courthouse, Butch showing up at my house. Anyone would need a drink after all that.

I unscrewed the cap.

The smell hit me first. Sharp, familiar, like coming home after a long trip. My mouth watered. My body remembered what my brain was trying to forget.

"Just one," I whispered. "Just to take the edge off."

I poured a small amount into a glass. Watched the clear liquid catch the kitchen light. I could almost feel the warmth spreading through my chest already, the loosening of the tight knot of anxiety that had lived in my stomach for months.

I brought the glass to my lips.

Somewhere in the back of my mind, Rachel's voice echoed. Call your sponsor. Call before you take that first drink. That's why I'm here.

But Rachel didn't understand. Rachel hadn't had her ex boyfriend try to kick down her door tonight. Rachel didn't know what it felt like to have the love of her life choose his daughter over her. Rachel didn't know.

I drank.

The burn was exquisite. It traced a line of fire down my throat and bloomed in my stomach like a flower opening. Within seconds, I felt my shoulders drop, felt my jaw unclench, felt the constant hum of anxiety quiet for the first time in months.

"Oh," I breathed. "Oh, I missed you."

I poured another. This one went down smoother. The third smoother still.

By the fourth, I had stopped counting. By the fifth, I had stopped caring.

The kitchen tilted slightly as I moved to the living room. I sank into the couch, the bottle now my companion, and let the numbness wash over me. No more Butch. No more Ricky. No more trial. No more protestors. No more failing at being a mother. No more pretending I could be someone I wasn't.

This was who I was. This was who I had always been. Why had I fought it so hard?

I don't remember falling asleep, but I woke to sunlight streaming through the windows and a pounding headache. The bottle was empty beside me on the couch. I was still in yesterday's clothes.

What time was it? I squinted at the clock. Nine thirty. Nine thirty?

The kids. School. Work. Mary's.

I stumbled to my feet, and the room spun. I grabbed the arm of the couch to steady myself. Okay. Okay. I just needed coffee. I just needed to splash water on my face. I could do this. I had done it before, plenty of times.

I made my way to the kitchen and found Mandy standing at the counter, her back to me. The little kids were at the table, eating cereal. They looked up when I entered.

"Mama!" Missy's face lit up, then fell. "Mama, are you okay? You look sick."

"I'm fine, baby. Just tired." My voice came out rough, scratchy. I cleared my throat. "Didn't sleep well."

Mandy turned around. Her face was stone.

"Missy, Davy, go to your room please."

"But I'm not done with my—"

"Now, Missy."

Something in Mandy's voice made both children obey without further argument. They slid off their chairs and padded down the hall. I heard their door close.

"Mandy, I can explain—"

"Can you?" She stepped closer. The hurt in her eyes was raw, anger barely contained beneath the surface. "Can you explain why there's an empty vodka bottle on the couch? Can you explain why you smell like a bar? Can you explain why, after everything, after all the promises, after all the progress, you did this again?"

"Butch was here last night. He tried to break down the door. I was scared, and I just needed—"

"You needed to call your sponsor. You needed to call me. You needed to do anything except this." Her voice cracked. "I knew not to trust you. You always do this. Give me false hope, and just when I think we are going to get past our issues... this."

"Mandy, please—"

"No." She held up her hand. "I can't do this anymore. I can't keep watching you destroy yourself. I can't keep explaining to Missy and Davy why Mama is sick again. I can't keep picking up the pieces."

"I'm sorry. I'm so sorry. It was just one night. I'll stop. I'll call Rachel. I'll—"

"You'll what? Go back to AA? Promise to do better? I've heard it all before, Mama. Every single time." Tears were streaming down her face now. "I wanted to believe you this time. I really did. You were doing so well, and I thought maybe, just maybe, we could actually be a family. But you can't even go one night without—"

She stopped, pressing her hand to her mouth. When she spoke again, her voice was barely a whisper.

"I'm taking the kids to Jimmy's."

"No. No, please, Mandy. Don't take them. I need them. I'll be better. I promise I'll be better."

"Your promises don't mean anything anymore."

She walked past me to the kids' room. I followed, stumbling, grabbing at the wall for support. My head was pounding, and my stomach churned with nausea and shame.

"Missy, Davy, we're going to go see daddy for a little while, okay? Pack your backpacks with some toys."

"Why, Mandy? I want to stay with Mama." Missy's lip trembled.

"Mama needs to rest, sweetie. She's not feeling well."

"Is it because of the bad man from last night? The one who was banging on the door?"

Mandy shot me a look. "Something like that. Come on, let's get your things."

I stood in the doorway, watching my children pack their little backpacks. Missy kept looking at me with those big worried eyes. Davy was quiet, clutching his stuffed tiger.

"Mama, you gonna be okay?" Missy asked.

I tried to smile. It felt grotesque on my face. "I'll be fine, baby. You go have fun with daddy."

"I don't wanna go." She ran to me and wrapped her arms around my legs. "I wanna stay with you, Mama. I can make you feel better. I can color you a picture."

The sob that escaped me was ugly, raw. I knelt down and held her, breathing in the scent of her shampoo, feeling her small heart beating against mine.

"I love you so much, Missy. I'm sorry. I'm so sorry."

"Why are you sorry, Mama?"

"I just am, baby. I love you."

Mandy gently pulled her away. "Come on, Missy. Daddy's waiting."

Little Davy toddled over to me. "Bye bye, Mama. Feel better." He patted my cheek with his small hand, and I thought my heart would shatter into a million pieces.

"Bye bye, sweet boy. I love you."

"Wuv you too."

And then they were gone. The door closed behind them, and I was alone.

The silence was deafening. I stood in the hallway, swaying slightly, staring at the door they had just walked through. My children. My babies. Gone again because of me. Because I couldn't resist one stupid bottle of vodka.

I made my way back to the living room and collapsed on the couch. The empty bottle mocked me from the coffee table. I needed more. I needed to make this feeling go away. The shame, the guilt, the look on Missy's face when she asked why I was sorry.

I couldn't drive. Even in my current state, I knew that. Not after the accident. Never again.

I picked up my phone, scrolling through contacts with blurry vision. Rachel. I should call Rachel. That's what I was supposed to do.

But Rachel would tell me to stop. Rachel would come over and pour out any alcohol she found and make me go to a meeting. Rachel would make me face this.

I didn't want to face this. I wanted to disappear into it.

My thumb stopped on a name I hadn't looked at in months. Jennifer.

Jennifer and I used to party together. Before Butch, before the accident, before everything. We'd close down bars and stumble home laughing. She never judged me. She never told me I had a problem. She just wanted to have fun.

I pressed call before I could change my mind.

"Hello?"

"Jen? It's Becca."

"Becca? Oh my God, girl, where have you been? I haven't heard from you in forever!"

"I know. I've been... going through some stuff."

"I heard about the accident. And all that mess with Butch. Girl, I'm so sorry. Are you okay?"

"No." My voice broke. "No, I'm not okay. Jen, I need... I need..."

"What do you need, honey? Name it."

"Can you come over? And can you bring... can you bring something to drink?"

There was a pause. "You sure? I heard you were doing the whole AA thing."

"I was. I'm not anymore. Please, Jen. I just need a friend right now. And a drink. Or ten."

She laughed, and it was a familiar sound, a sound from my old life. "Say no more, babe. I'll be there in twenty. We'll have a girls' night like old times. Just what the doctor ordered."

"Thank you. Thank you, Jen."

"Of course, honey. That's what friends are for."

I hung up and let the phone drop to the cushion beside me. Twenty minutes. I could survive twenty minutes.

I closed my eyes and waited for my old friend to arrive with my old friend in a bottle.

When Jennifer knocked, I practically ran to the door. She stood there with a huge grin and a paper bag clinking with promise.

"Oh honey, you look terrible." She pulled me into a hug. "Let's fix that."

She breezed past me into the living room, pulling bottles from the bag like a magician pulling rabbits from a hat. Vodka, rum, tequila. She had come prepared.

"I didn't know what you were in the mood for, so I brought options." She winked at me. "Now tell me everything. What happened with that psycho ex of yours? I heard he showed up here last night?"

"How did you know?"

"Girl, this is Glenn Lake. Everyone knows everything five minutes after it happens." She poured two generous glasses of vodka. "Here. Drink up. You look like you need it."

I took the glass. My second drink in less than twelve hours, after five months of sobriety. The voice in my head, the one that sounded like Rachel, was getting quieter.

"So spill. What's going on? Besides the obvious Butch drama."

And I did. I spilled everything. Ricky coming back into my life, Mandy finally starting to trust me, the bakery job, the recovery, and then it all falling apart. Ricky ending things, Amelia hating me, Butch at the courthouse, Butch at my house, Mandy taking the kids.

With each revelation, Jennifer refilled my glass. With each refill, the pain got duller, further away, like watching it happen to someone else on a television screen.

"Men are trash," Jennifer declared after I finished telling her about Ricky. "All of them. You don't need him."

"But I love him."

"So? Love is overrated. You know what's not overrated? This." She held up her glass. "This never lets you down. This is always there for you."

I laughed, and it felt good to laugh, even if it was hollow. "You're right. You're absolutely right."

"Of course I am. Now come on, let's put on some music and forget about all these losers."

She found some old playlist on her phone, songs from our bar hopping days, and suddenly we were dancing in my living room, drinks sloshing, laughing like we were twenty three again with no responsibilities, no kids, no exes trying to kill us.

At some point, the first bottle was empty, and we opened the second. At some point, the dancing stopped and we were just sitting on the floor, backs against the couch, passing the bottle between us.

"I missed you, Bec," Jennifer slurred. "You were so boring when you were sober."

"I was trying to be a good mom."

"You were miserable. I could tell. Every time I saw you at the grocery store or whatever, you looked so sad. Like a caged animal. This is the real you. The fun you."

Was she right? Was this the real me? Maybe the sober Becca was the fake one. Maybe all that progress was just pretending to be someone I wasn't.

The room was spinning now, but I didn't care. I welcomed it. The spinning meant I wasn't thinking. The spinning meant I couldn't feel.

"I'm gonna be sick," I announced, and Jennifer just laughed and pointed me toward the bathroom.

I don't remember much after that. Flashes of throwing up. Flashes of crying on the bathroom floor. Flashes of Jennifer leaving at some point, promising to come back tomorrow with more supplies.

I woke up sometime the next day, face down on the living room carpet, head splitting, mouth like sandpaper. The house smelled like alcohol and vomit and regret.

But instead of stopping, instead of calling Rachel or Mandy or anyone who could help me, I crawled to where Jennifer had left the tequila and took another drink.

If I was going to destroy everything I'd built, I might as well do it thoroughly.

Chapter Twenty

I woke up on the living room floor, cheek pressed against the carpet, mouth dry as sand. The light coming through the windows was too bright, stabbing at my eyes like needles.

What day was it? How long had I been like this?

I tried to push myself up, but my arms shook so badly I collapsed back down. My stomach lurched, and I had to breathe through my nose to keep from being sick right there on the floor.

"What is that smell?" I muttered. Then I realized. It was me.

I lay there for a long moment, taking inventory. I was wearing one sock and a tank top that was twisted around backward, and nothing else. My hair was matted to my face. There were bottles scattered around the room, some empty, some knocked over with sticky puddles beneath them.

The house was destroyed. Cushions thrown off the couch. A lamp knocked over. What looked like the remnants of the food Caroline had brought splattered across the wall and floor. Had I thrown it? I couldn't remember.

"What the hell have I done?"

The question hung in the air, unanswered. I knew exactly what I had done. I had thrown away five months of sobriety. I had scared my children. I had confirmed every terrible thing Mandy had ever thought about me.

I collapsed into a pile of tears and cried my heart out on the living room floor. I had broken all my promises. I was a horrible person. I really did have to get myself together. I had hit rock bottom again. All I could do was dig up again. Zero days since my last drink and counting.

I let myself lay there and wallow for an hour or so, letting myself mourn and belittle myself for my relapse. Flashes of memory kept surfacing. Jennifer laughing as she poured another drink. Dancing in the living room. Throwing up in the bathroom. Waking up alone and reaching for the tequila instead of my phone.

And before all that, the memories that hurt the most. Missy wrapping her arms around my legs, not wanting to leave. "I can color you a picture, Mama." Little Davy patting my cheek. "Feel better."

Mandy's face, hard as stone, tears streaming down her cheeks. "I knew not to trust you. You always do this."

Mandy wouldn't forgive me this time. I had let her down one too many times, and I had said so many horrible things. I couldn't even remember what all I had said when Jennifer was here, but I knew drunk me. Drunk me was mean. Drunk me said things sober me would never say.

"Oh, Mandy, I'm so very sorry." I said to the empty room. "I promise, this time, I won't do it again."

I wanted to believe it. I didn't want to keep letting her down. This time I knew what was at stake and what I stood to lose. That's the difference between my past and now. I didn't want this drunk life. I wanted my family.

First things first, I needed to take a shower and then start cleaning my mess. I stood slowly, waiting for the room to stop spinning, and scanned the destruction around me.

It was awful. I had so much rage, and the alcohol unleashed it all. I shook my head and headed down the hall to my shower.

I gasped when my reflection came into view. I looked like death warmed over. Hair matted, bloodshot eyes, and I looked aged. Like I had lived ten years in the span of three days.

I turned on the hot water and let it warm as I stripped out of the minimal clothing I was wearing. Shame washed over me as I stepped into the shower. I stood under the water as a fresh batch of tears formed.

How many times had I stood in this exact spot, washing away the evidence of another binge? How many times had I promised myself this was the last time? The water ran over my face, mixing with my tears until I couldn't tell which was which.

I thought about Missy's face when she asked why I was sorry. I thought about Davy saying "wuv you" as Mandy led him out the door. I thought about all the moments I had missed with Mandy when she was their age, all the moments I had sworn I wouldn't miss with them.

And here I was, missing them again. By choice. Because I was too weak to put down a bottle.

I washed my hair then my body, scrubbing hard like I could scrub away my sins. I continued to stand under the hot water long after I was clean. The rush of water felt like the only good thing in my life right now.

How was I going to fix my relationship with my children this time? Words wouldn't be enough. I needed to make a plan and then stick with it. Maybe increase my counseling sessions and work on my coping techniques. Maybe actually call Rachel when I felt the urge instead of calling Jennifer.

I turned off the water, grabbing a towel. This time when I saw my reflection, it looked slightly better. Still haggard. Still ashamed. But cleaner. I ran a brush through my hair, working through the tangles until it was smooth again.

After I dressed in clean clothes, I gathered up all my dirty laundry and started a load. Then I got to work on the rest of the mess.

I started in the living room, picking up bottles first. I counted them as I dropped them into a trash bag. One, two, three, four. Four bottles in three days. No wonder I felt like I was dying.

I scrubbed at the carpet where something had spilled. I wiped down the walls where I had apparently thrown Caroline's food. I righted the lamp and put the cushions back on the couch.

With each act of cleaning, I tried to call Mandy. Each time, it rang straight to voicemail.

"Hi, baby, it's Mama. Please call me back. I'm so sorry. I just want to talk."

Voicemail.

"Mandy, please. I know you're angry, and you have every right to be. Just let me explain."

Voicemail.

"I'm not drinking anymore. I'm cleaning up. Please, just call me."

Voicemail.

I stopped leaving messages after the fifth one. She wasn't going to call. She was done with me. I couldn't blame her.

I kept cleaning anyway. It gave me something to do besides think. Besides feel. The house slowly began to look like a home again instead of the aftermath of a tornado.

"Oh my gosh, I screwed up big time," I said as I scrubbed at a particularly stubborn stain on the floor.

I was having a hard time facing things without Ricky. It was stupid, but I loved him. I knew that I shouldn't depend on him for my happiness, but he had been such a support to me in so many low points in my life. My heart and soul needed his for comfort. He was my other half in so many ways.

But he had ended things. He had chosen Amelia over me, and I understood why, but understanding didn't make it hurt less. Understanding didn't fill the hole in my chest where he used to be.

I had a lot of apologies to make, starting with Mary. When I had tried to go to work drunk on the second day, she had just looked at me with such sadness. No anger. Just disappointment and concern. She told me to take time to get myself together. She didn't fire me, but she also didn't make me feel like everything was okay.

Maybe that hurt my feelings more. I expected everyone to get mad, but she didn't. Instead, she hugged me before sending me away. I needed her to see me sober and remorseful.

Then there was Caroline. She had brought me food, trying to help, and I had snapped at her and thrown things. She just smiled sadly and left the food on the porch. After she left, I had thrown it all over the living room like a toddler having a tantrum.

Thinking about her now, I sobbed harder as I cleaned up the last of that mess. I owed her a lot of apologies. She was so sweet and always had my back. So why was my instinct to push people away? I knew the answer, but I still asked it. It wasn't an excuse to act out.

I stood back and looked at the living room. It was clean now. You would never know that three days ago it had looked like a war zone. But the evidence of what I had done wasn't just in the mess. It was in the empty house. The silence where my children's voices should be.

I wouldn't blame any of my friends or family if they never spoke to me ever again.

I tried Mandy one more time. Voicemail.

I stared at my phone for a long moment. There was someone else I needed to call. Someone I should have called three days ago instead of Jennifer.

My thumb hovered over Rachel's name. Part of me wanted to put it off, to wait until I felt stronger, more put together. But that was the old Becca. The old Becca who hid and avoided and let shame fester into something worse.

I pressed call before I could talk myself out of it.

She answered on the second ring. "Becca?"

"Rachel, I..." My voice cracked. "I have to confess something."

"I'm listening." No judgment in her tone. Just steady, patient presence.

"I relapsed. Three days ago. Butch showed up at my house, tried to break down my door, and I just... I gave in. I drank. A lot." The words tumbled out, ugly and raw. "I didn't call you. I called an old drinking buddy instead, and we... I lost three days, Rachel. Three whole days. My kids are gone. Mandy took them to their father's, and she won't even answer my calls."

Silence on the other end. I braced myself for disappointment, for the lecture I deserved.

"Are you sober now?" Rachel asked gently.

"Yes. Since this morning. I cleaned up the house. I've been trying to reach Mandy, but..." I couldn't finish.

"Becca, listen to me. You relapsed. It happens. It doesn't erase the five months you had. It doesn't make you a failure. It makes you human."

"But I was doing so well. I thought I was past this."

"Recovery isn't a straight line. You know that. The question isn't whether you fell. The question is whether you're going to get back up."

The tears came then, hot and fast. Relief and shame all tangled together. "I want to. I really do. I just don't know if anyone will believe me this time."

"I believe you. And that's enough for right now. One person believing in you. One hour at a time. One day at a time. That's how we do this."

I sobbed into the phone, unable to form words. Rachel just waited, letting me cry, not rushing me or trying to fix it. Just being there.

"Thank you," I finally managed. "Thank you for not giving up on me."

"That's what sponsors are for. Now, tomorrow I want you at a meeting. Can you do that?"

"Yes."

"Good. And Becca? Call me anytime. Day or night. That's why I gave you my number. Use it next time, okay?"

"I will. I promise."

After we hung up, I felt something shift in my chest. The shame was still there, but it wasn't alone anymore. There was a tiny spark of something else. Hope, maybe. Or at least the possibility of hope.

I set my phone down and took a deep breath.

There was a knock at the door.

My heart leaped. Mandy? Had she come back? Had she decided to give me another chance?

I walked to the door, trying to smooth down my hair, trying to look like someone worthy of forgiveness. I took a deep breath and opened it.

It wasn't Mandy.

"Oh, Ricky, what are you doing here?"

He stood on my porch, looking at me with those dark eyes full of concern and something else. Love. Still love, after everything.

"I need to apologize to you. I'm so sorry that I walked away and wasn't there for you. Love is supposed to be dependable. Love is always there." He stepped forward and wrapped his arms around me.

Fresh tears fell. I didn't even know I was crying at first. I just felt his arms around me, solid and warm and real, and something inside me cracked open.

"Ricky... oh, Ricky, I screwed up so badly. I lost my children again." I said, trying to breathe through the sobs. "I... Butch came back, and it was just the excuse I needed to give in to the urge. Please don't leave me again, please."

"I'm here. I'm here." He pulled me tighter as he started to cry too.

We stumbled inside together, still holding each other, and somehow ended up on the floor. We melted together into a pile of tears on the living room carpet I had just scrubbed clean. We held each other as we wept, going back and forth between apologizing and comforting the other.

"I'm sorry I ended things," he said into my hair. "I was trying to make Amelia happy, but I was miserable. And then I heard about

Butch coming here, and I couldn't... I couldn't stand the thought of you going through that alone."

"How did you know?"

"My mom told me. She heard from Sheriff Riley. And then Darla said something about Missy telling her you got drunk and the kids had to go to Jimmy's, and I just... I had to come. I had to see you."

"I'm such a mess, Ricky. Look at me. I'm not the person you fell in love with."

He pulled back and cupped my face in his hands, looking at me with such tenderness it made my chest ache.

"You're exactly the person I fell in love with. You're struggling, yes. But you're still you. You're still Becca. And I still love you."

"How can you love me after this? After everything?"

"Because love isn't about being perfect. It's about being there. And I wasn't there for you, and I'm sorry. But I'm here now. And I'm not leaving again."

We sat there on the floor for a long time, holding each other. By the end of the crying session, we kissed. We laughed a little, that shaky laugh that comes after you've cried yourself empty. And we said I love you.

"Becca, I am here for you now and will support you through your recovery. We will get through it all together." He kissed my head. "Mandy will forgive you. You're a good person that just had a rough life."

"I don't know. I screwed up one time too many. She won't even answer my calls."

"No, I think she will forgive you again. She loves you. She's just scared and hurt right now."

"I hope you're right. I'm so scared that if any little stress comes my way, I will relapse again. I thought I was stronger than this. Five months, Ricky. I had five months."

"And you'll have five months again. And then six. And then a year. I plan to make it easier from here on out. I can't promise perfect, but I can promise I am here for you and will never leave you again."

"Oh, Ricky, I love you." I leaned into him, letting myself believe, just for a moment, that things might actually be okay.

"I love you too. Now." He stood and offered me his hand. "Let's go get your kids back."

My stomach clenched with fear. "What if she won't talk to me? What if she slams the door in my face?"

"Then we'll wait on the porch until she's ready. However long it takes. You're not doing this alone anymore, Becca. We're doing it together."

I took his hand and let him pull me to my feet. Together. I had forgotten what that word felt like.

"Okay," I said, my voice shaky but determined. "Let's go."

We headed out to his car together. I didn't know what was waiting for me at Jimmy's house. I didn't know if Mandy would forgive me. But for the first time in three days, I had hope.

And I wasn't alone.

Chapter Twenty-One

The drive to Jimmy's felt like the longest ten minutes of my life. I sat in the passenger seat, hands clasped tightly in my lap, watching the familiar streets of Glenn Lake pass by the window. My stomach was in knots.

"I'm nervous. What if I ruined our relationship? We had finally gotten so close." I put my head in my hands and tried not to get sick in his car.

Ricky reached over and squeezed my knee. "It's going to be okay. Just be honest with her. That's all you can do."

We pulled up in front of Jimmy's house. It was a modest brick home with a well kept yard. I had been here dozens of times to drop off the kids or pick them up, but it had never felt this intimidating before.

I got out of the car slowly and made my way up the driveway to the front door. Ricky walked beside me but hung back a little, giving me space. This was my conversation to have.

Before I could knock, the door opened. Mandy stood there, arms crossed over her chest, face unreadable. She must have seen us pull up.

"Hi."

"Hi, Mama. How are you?" Her voice was flat, guarded.

"I'm better. I just... I have no excuse. I'm just sorry, Mandy." I hung my head, unable to meet her eyes.

"Why should I think this time will be different, Mama? You say this every time." She didn't move from the doorway, didn't invite me in.

"I don't know what to say other than I'm sorry."

"This was ugly. I hope you know what you have put us through. You scared us. And you let me down big time. I trusted you." Her voice cracked on the last word, and I saw a flash of the hurt beneath her anger.

"I know. I know. There is nothing I can say to make this better. I will just have to show you I am trying." I finally looked up at her. "And look, your dad..."

Ricky was walking towards us. He and Mandy exchanged a look, a nod of acknowledgment between father and daughter.

"Mandy, I know this is a setback for you all. I know I started it by breaking up for the dumbest reason, but I'm here to support her, you, and the recovery for you both. I have faith in all of us getting past this. Second chances, third chances, whatever it takes for us to be a family."

"It wasn't just the breakup," I added quickly. "It was so many things. The protestors, the trial, two run ins with Butch, counseling... I could go on, but I have no excuse. I just... I love you, Mandy. Please, I want to show you I can do this. I'm trying."

Mandy looked back and forth between us, processing what we were both saying. The war happening behind her eyes was plain to see. The part of her that wanted to protect herself, to keep me at arm's length where I couldn't hurt her again. And the part of her that still wanted her mother.

Finally, she exhaled and dropped her crossed arms.

"Mama, I love you. I know this isn't easy for you." She paused. "I will try too."

The sob that escaped me was pure relief. I stepped forward and wrapped my arms around her, holding her tight. There were more tears, hers and mine, soaking into each other's shoulders.

"Thank you," I whispered. "Thank you for giving me another chance. I won't waste it this time."

"You better not." But there was a hint of warmth in her voice now, a crack in the wall she had built.

Ricky watched us for a moment, then stepped forward and wrapped his arms around us both. The three of us stood there in Jimmy's doorway, a tangle of tears and forgiveness and hope.

When we finally pulled apart, Ricky kept one arm around me and looked at Mandy with an expression I couldn't quite read.

"I still need to talk to Amelia too, but if she is on board, I want to make this right..." He paused, and then he reached into his pocket and dropped to one knee. "Will you marry me, Becca?"

I gasped. Mandy gasped. We looked at each other with wide eyes, then back at Ricky, who was holding up a ring. It was beautiful, a simple band with a modest diamond that caught the light.

"Are you serious? After this past week?"

"Yes, I am serious. I love you, Becca, and I want to marry you. I've loved you since you were fourteen years old. I don't want to waste any more time."

"Yes," I said, my voice trembling. "Yes, of course. But I need to know that Amelia is okay with this too. I know it won't be easy for her, but I am willing to try."

He slid the ring onto my finger and stood, pulling me into a kiss. When we broke apart, Mandy was crying and smiling at the same time.

"I can't believe this is happening," she said. "My parents are getting married."

"Well, should we head to Maria and Carl's to talk to my kids?" Ricky asked.

"Yes, but first, I need to see Missy and Little Davy. Do you think they are still scared of me? I know my behavior scared them."

Mandy's face softened. "They have been asking for you. They know you are sick, and I told them you had to get well, just like when they had a cold over the winter."

We stepped inside the house. It smelled like coffee and laundry detergent, normal and comforting. I barely had time to look around before I heard the pounding of small feet.

"Mama!"

Missy came running down the hallway and threw herself into my arms. I caught her and held her tight, burying my face in her hair, breathing in the scent of her strawberry shampoo. My baby. My sweet girl.

"I missed you so much, Mama. You look so much better now! I was worried about you."

"I'm feeling better, baby. I'm so sorry I scared you."

"It's okay. I knew you would get better. I prayed for you." She pulled back and looked at me with those big serious eyes. "Mandy explained that you have a sickness that makes you want to drink grown up drinks even when they make you act not like yourself. Is that true?"

Leave it to Mandy to find a way to explain addiction to a five year old. "Yes, baby. That's true. But I'm working really hard to get better."

"Good. Because I like you better when you're yourself." She hugged me again.

Little Davy had been hanging back, watching from behind Jimmy's legs. He was more cautious than his sister, more sensitive to moods and tension. I held out my hand to him.

"Hey, sweet boy. Can I have a hug?"

He looked at me for a long moment, then toddled over. I scooped him up and held both my babies, one in each arm, and let the tears fall.

"I'm so sorry. I let you both down again."

"It's okay, Mama," Missy said, her voice muffled against my shoulder.

"No, it's not. I should have been able to control myself, and I'll try really hard to do that going forward."

"Okay, Mama. Can we go home now?"

I looked up at Mandy and Jimmy for confirmation. They exchanged a glance, some silent communication passing between them, and then both nodded.

"Soon, baby. I think you'll stay with daddy one more night. Mama needs to take care of a few things first."

"Okay." She hugged me one more time.

"I wuv you, Mama." Davy patted my cheek, just like he had three days ago when they left. But this time, there was no sadness in his eyes. Just love.

"I love you too, Little Davy. I love you both so much."

After we said our goodbyes, with promises that I would see them tomorrow, Ricky and I headed to his car. The ring on my finger caught the afternoon light, and I still couldn't quite believe it was there.

"Are you ready for this?" Ricky asked as he started the engine.

"No," I admitted. "But let's do it anyway."

We rode to Maria and Carl's without talking much, just the sound of the road and the radio. Ricky placed his hand on my knee and squeezed it lightly for comfort as we pulled up at the house.

He knocked and walked in. Maria appeared in the foyer almost immediately.

"Ricky? I thought you were working." She looked past him and saw me. "Hi, Becca. I heard what happened with your ex. Are you okay?" She pulled me into a hug before I could answer.

"Thanks, I'm okay. Now." I smiled at Ricky.

"I need to talk to my kids," he said.

"I have nothing to say to you with her here. She's just a drunk."

I turned to find Amelia standing in the doorway to the living room. Her arms were crossed, her jaw set, looking so much like her father when he was being stubborn.

"Amelia, you do not talk about her like that. You have to have respect for adults."

"I knew you would take her back. You're a liar." She turned and ran out of the room.

Ricky started to go after her, but then he stopped and turned back to me.

"I should tell you something before you go in there." He ran a hand through his hair, looking tired. "I've been talking to Amelia a lot these past few weeks. About her mom, about grief, about what it means to let new people into our lives. Maria's been helping too, and we even did a few sessions with a family counselor."

"I didn't know that."

"She's been making progress. Real progress. But it's slow, and some days are harder than others." He glanced toward the hallway where Amelia had disappeared. "The thing is, it's not really about you, Becca. Not personally. She's terrified that loving someone new means forgetting her mother. She's scared that if I'm happy, it means I didn't love her mom enough. It's all tangled up in her grief."

"That makes sense. I felt something similar after my parents died, even though we weren't close."

"She told me last week that she wants me to be happy. She said it in this small voice, like she was admitting something she felt guilty about. I think part of her is ready to try. She just needs to know that trying won't cost her anything. That there's room for all of it."

I nodded slowly, understanding settling over me. This wasn't a battle I needed to win. It was a relationship that needed patience and gentleness and time.

"Let me go talk to her," I said, putting my hand on his arm.

I didn't know yet what I was going to say, but I knew I had to step up, or she would never accept me. There was no guarantee she would even if I talked to her, but I had to try.

She had gone down the hall to a spare bedroom and was face down on the bed, crying. I knocked softly on the door frame, but she didn't look at me.

"Amelia, I know I'm the last person you want to talk to you, but please hear me out." Her crying paused slightly, like she was actually going to listen. I took that as permission to continue.

"I know I haven't been the best person in my life. I have made a lot of mistakes. I have done things I'm not proud of. I know you have heard rumors, and yes, some of the things are true, but not everything is true."

I paused to gather my thoughts. This was the most important conversation I might ever have. I needed to get it right.

"I don't want to take your mom's place. I never could. Nothing can replace a mother. I have heard a lot about her from your dad. She sounds like an amazing mother, and I am so sorry you lost her at only seven years old. That is so unfair."

She turned and looked at me, her eyes red and puffy. So, I continued.

"I lost my mother when I was twenty-three years old. And even though she was a horrible mother to me, I think about her every day. If she would have been as amazing a mother as yours, I just can't even imagine how much harder that loss would be." I moved closer, sitting on the edge of the bed. "So, Amelia, I hope you will give me a chance. Just get to know me for me. Not the rumors, not the person you think is trying to steal your dad or take your mother's place. Please, just give me a chance."

She didn't move or make a sound. She stayed perfectly still, staring at me. I waited. I was patient. Ricky was worth this. I had waited nineteen years to be with him again. I could wait a few minutes to get a reaction from his eight-year-old daughter.

I needed her approval. Not just for him, but for myself as well. I wanted this family to work. I wanted all our kids to grow up together, to be siblings in every way that mattered.

Finally, she spoke.

"I'm sorry about your mother too." She sat up slowly, wiping her eyes with the back of her hand. "I... I guess I can give you a chance. I mean, I don't want my daddy to be unhappy, and Aunt Maria said he loves you very much. She said he deserves to be happy, and I do want him to be." She paused. "Mandy and Darla like you. I trust them."

A half smile crossed her face, tentative but real.

"Thank you, Amelia. That means more to me than you know. I hope that I can get you to trust me too and that we can be friends someday."

"I will try." She paused and then looked up at me again, her eyes meeting mine directly for the first time. "I promise to try."

"I promise to try too."

I held out my hand, and she shook it solemnly, like we were sealing a business deal. I guess in a way, we were.

We both turned to see Ricky standing in the doorway, tears streaming down his face. We all kind of gave one of those nervous laughs, the tension breaking.

"Come here, you two," he said, and we all hugged. It was awkward and new and imperfect, but it was a start.

Later that night, alone in my house with my guy, I reflected on the last several months. It had not been easy, but it was worth all the hard work. I looked down at Ricky. He was sleeping peacefully, his face relaxed in a way I rarely saw when he was awake.

I smiled and settled in closer to him. He reached out even in sleep and pulled me even closer, turning to wrap his body around me.

"I love you, Becca," he murmured.

"I love you too, Ricky."

I lay there in the darkness, listening to him breathe, feeling the ring on my finger. Tomorrow I would call Rachel and tell her about my relapse. Tomorrow I would go back to AA and start over. Tomorrow I would face Mary and Caroline and apologize for everything.

Tomorrow would bring its challenges. Butch's trial was scheduled for three months from now, and I would have to face him again, this time in a courtroom full of people. The DA seemed confident, especially after Butch violated his bail conditions by coming to my house. Between that and the original charges, he would likely spend years behind bars. Maybe the rest of his life.

I used to be terrified of that day. The thought of seeing him again, of having to testify about that night, had been one of the shadows that pushed me toward the bottle. But lying here now, with Ricky's arm around me and the knowledge that I wouldn't be facing it alone, the fear felt smaller. Manageable.

It wouldn't be easy. Nothing about recovery ever was. But I had survived so much already. I could survive a courtroom too.

But tonight, I let myself feel something I hadn't felt in a very long time.

Peace.

I finally felt my soul smile, and all the ghosts of my past began to fade.

~ ~

"Hi, my name is Becca. I have been sober for one year now. I am here today to share my story. It's a story of survival, overcoming obstacles, and finding myself."

THE END

Before you go: If you loved Becca's Story, be sure to visit my website to sign up for my newsletter (if you haven't already) and to stay up to date on new releases and other bookish things.

When signing up, you will receive **Chef Jessica's Alphabet Soup Recipe** as a free gift. I have "had" it; it is yummy. (Okay, so obviously, it is my recipe, but still, I recommend it!)

Continue to the next section for this book's recipe!

Also, check out my other books! You can find links on my website.

www.ejwheltonwrites.com

Author note:

There is a lot of narration in this book. As a reader myself, I know that a lot of time in the character's head can get boring; however, I wanted to show the loneliness that is a huge part of being a single parent. Even with the support of others, every decision, every minute, is about the children and what makes sense for them.

While the story itself is fiction, much of the inspiration came from my own struggles with being a single parent, caring for my kids, and balancing their needs while dating. I felt like there were days I didn't even talk to another human besides myself.

Thank you for taking the time to read my story. I enjoy sharing my ideas with others.

Thank you, and happy reading!

For more information about this and my other work, please visit my website:

www.ejwheltonwrites.com